Anything but
Normal

Anything but Normal

A Novel

Melody Carlson

Revell

a division of Baker Publishing Group
Grand Rapids, Michigan

© 2010 by Melody Carlson

Published by Revell
a division of Baker Publishing Group
P.O. Box 6287, Grand Rapids, MI 49516-6287
www.revellbooks.com

Printed in the United States of America

Library of Congress Cataloging-in-Publication Data
Carlson, Melody.
        Anything but normal : a novel / Melody Carlson.
            p.   cm.
        Summary: Honor student and future journalist Sophie, a seventeen-year-old
    senior, was pressured to break her purity pledge and fears she is pregnant, but is
    unable to go to her parents, friends, pastor, or even God for help.
        ISBN 978-0-8007-3258-5 (pbk.)
        [1. Secrets—Fiction. 2. Pregnancy—Fiction. 3. Christian life—Fiction. 4. High
    schools—Fiction. 5. Schools—Fiction. 6. Journalism—Fiction.] I. Title.
    PZ7.C216637Any 2010
    [Fic]—dc22   2009025389

10   11   12   13   14   15   16   7 6 5 4 3 2 1

1

"Whaddya think, Sophie?" Carrie Anne stepped out of the fitting room and performed a quick 360-degree turn. She patted the backside of the slim-fitting jeans and then frowned. "Do these make my trunk look big?"

Sophie rolled her eyes. "Yeah, right. Your trunk belongs on a Matchbox car"—she turned her own rear end toward her best friend—"whereas mine is more like the back end of a Club Cab."

Carrie Anne laughed. "Hey, lots of guys appreciate a little junk in the trunk."

"Enough with the car metaphors." Sophie stared at her own image in the three-way mirror and groaned. "This is so useless. And these jeans are the worst ones yet. Seriously, I give up."

"It's just that the pockets are all wrong." Carrie Anne pointed to Sophie's behind. "See, they should be lower down and set farther apart—it's just a bad design."

"Or maybe I'm just a bad design."

Carrie Anne gave Sophie a stern look. "Okay, now you're insulting the designer."

"No, I didn't mean it like that. Besides, it's not God's fault that I'm fat. I mean, I wasn't born fat."

"You're *not* fat, Sophie."

"Uh-huh." Sophie turned away. Carrie Anne's definition of "fat" was pretty subjective, not to mention contradictory. She'd try to convince Sophie that she wasn't overweight, but if her own waist developed the slightest muffin top over a pair of size 2 jeans, she had no problem saying, "Oh, man, I'm such a porker. I need to lose ten pounds." And then Carrie Anne would launch into the latest, greatest lose-weight-fast tips— kind of like "hint hint."

"You're just *curvy*." Carrie Anne continued with her passive-aggressive routine. Really, Sophie was used to this stuff, so why let it get to her now?

"Yeah, whatever." Sophie reached for the door as the lump in her throat grew larger.

"Don't be so hard on yourself."

"Right." Sophie went into the dressing room and locked the door behind her. Tears were sneaking out and trickling down her flushed face. What was wrong with her? When had she turned into such a wimp?

"Why don't you let me pick out another pair for you?" Carrie Anne called out. "I saw some jeans that—"

"That's okay." Sophie pulled up the bottom of her baggy Gap shirt, using the hem to dry her cheeks. Of course, this simply revealed the overly plump muffin top that was pouring over the waist of her too-small jeans. "I think I've tried on enough clothes for today, Carrie."

"But school starts on Tuesday."

"And your point is?" Sophie popped open the button and released the zipper, allowing her tummy to spill out and her lungs to inhale properly. Seriously, overly tight jeans had to be hazardous to one's health. Manufacturers should be forced to put a warning label on them.

"What are you going to wear next week?"

"The same things I'm wearing this week."

Carrie Anne didn't respond.

"Don't worry." Sophie tried to insert some cheer into her voice. "I'll try not to look like a bag lady." She peeled off the detestable pants, then stared blankly into the full-length mirror in front of her. Some of her friends thought she looked like Drew Barrymore. But today Sophie thought she looked . . . well, generally unimpressive. Her honey-colored, shoulder-length hair was pulled back into a sloppy ponytail. Her greenish blue eyes, one of her better features, looked swollen and red. And her turned-up nose, also red, was dripping. She used the hem of her shirt again. Really, she should listen to her mom and start carrying tissues in her purse.

Sophie stood up straight, taking in another deep breath. This was so out of character for her. So perfectly ridiculous. She really needed to pull herself together. Sure, she was pleasantly plump. But good grief, that was nothing new. She'd begun developing curves way back in fifth grade. That had been torturous enough back then—her peers had still looked like spindly colts while she'd felt like a clumsy cow. But now that she was seventeen and a senior, her friends had finally caught up. Or nearly. Carrie Anne's bra size was still a teeny-weeny 32AA. And even though she claimed it was 34A, Sophie knew better because she had recently seen one of Carrie Anne's bras on top of a laundry basket and checked it.

Sophie squared her shoulders and decided to take a more positive inventory of her appearance. Seriously, it was time to count her blessings, to be thankful for how God had made her. For one thing, she was able to walk, and her mind still worked okay. Not that it was much consolation.

She shook her head and took another good look at her image in the mirror. At least she was still sporting a pretty good tan, the result of spending all of August working at the church youth camp. And her legs were actually in pretty good shape. Running up and down all those trails, trying to keep up with the crazy middle school girls, had paid off.

"Hey, Sophie, you coming outta there anytime soon?" Carrie Anne asked.

Sophie grabbed up her cargo pants. "Yeah, I'm still getting dressed."

"I'm going to get that last pair of jeans I tried on. Meet me at the cash register, okay?"

"Sounds good." Sophie pulled on her loose pants. The well-worn fabric felt cool and soft against her skin, fantastic compared to that last pair of horrid jeans. She slipped into her Banana Republic flip-flops and reached for her bag. Carrie Anne would probably appreciate it if Sophie fixed up her face a bit. Besides, who knew whom she might run into here at the mall? So she put on some fresh lip gloss, adjusted her smudged mascara, and even removed the haphazard ponytail, brushing and fluffing out her naturally wavy hair. There, much better.

Carrie Anne juggled her shopping bags, holding up her latest purchase like a trophy as the cashier placed her change on the counter. "I'm almost out of money now."

"Big surprise there."

"And I'm starving." Carrie Anne dropped one of her sacks. "Ready for lunch?"

Sophie picked up the fallen bag. "Need some help with those?"

"Yeah." Carrie Anne shoved the largest bag toward Sophie—it was from Macy's and looked like it was about to fall apart. "Take this one too. It's what you get for not buying anything yourself."

"Maybe I'll find something after lunch." Sophie rearranged her purse to accommodate the oversized bag. "And next time I'll try one size bigger."

"Or . . . ," Carrie Anne's voice sounded cautious, ". . . you could get a really great pair of jeans that are one size too small and use them as an incentive to shed a couple of pounds."

Sophie nodded. "Yeah . . . I guess that could work." But even as she said this, she knew it was ridiculous. Carrie Anne and her mom were always full of "great" ideas for losing weight. The problem was, although they seemed to work for Carrie Anne and her mom, they never worked for Sophie. Normally Sophie didn't really care all that much. Normally she was pretty okay with herself. Normally she could make jokes about these things. But for some reason, today felt anything but normal.

Maybe that was why Sophie took her best friend's hint and ordered carefully for lunch. Low cal, low carb, and low appeal. When they finally found an available table right in the center of the food court, still cluttered with lunch debris and spilled soda, Sophie sat down and frowned at her lunch. A boring green salad topped with a few anorexic-looking chicken strips. Suddenly she found herself lusting after cheeseburgers, pepperoni pizza, and Carrie Anne's crispy meat burrito and Mexi fries. Still, she tried not to show it as she unfolded her paper napkin and pasted a smile on her face.

"So what're you doing for Labor Day?" Carrie Anne asked.

"Mom's driving Bart back to school and won't be back until Tuesday." Sophie forked a piece of lettuce. "And Dad plans to keep the tire store open on Monday. Like he thinks everyone and their grandmother will be out shopping for retreads or tire chains that day." Sophie sighed. "The truth is, he'll be sitting there watching some lame ball game, pretending to work. Seriously, he needs to join a twelve-step group for ESPN addiction."

"Why don't you come out to the lake with us?" Carrie Anne picked up her burrito and took a big bite.

Sophie nodded. "Sure. That sounds great."

"The Stewarts and the Morrises will be bringing their boats too."

Sophie stopped chewing. The chunk of chicken in her mouth suddenly felt like wood, and when she tried to swallow, it seemed to get stuck in her throat. Panicking, she took a quick gulp of iced tea, then nearly choked. Coughing and sputtering, she covered her mouth with her hands and wondered if she was about to suffocate.

"Are you okay, Sophie?"

She finally swallowed the hard lump of chicken, took a deep breath followed by a careful swig of tea, then nodded with watery eyes. "I'm fine," she said in a husky voice.

"Man, I was about ready to do the Heimlich on you."

"Thanks." Sophie pushed her half-eaten salad away from her.

"Seriously, are you okay?"

"I said *I'm fine.*"

Carrie Anne blinked. "Well, you don't have to get mad."

"I'm not mad." Sophie focused her attention on folding her napkin into neat triangles, over and over. Kind of like origami, only fatter.

"So anyway, the Stewarts and Morrises will be there, which reminds me"—she shook her finger at Sophie—"you never told me that Dylan Morris was up at Camp Calderwood."

Sophie shrugged, avoiding Carrie's gaze. "What's to tell?"

Carrie Anne leaned forward. "Well, you know I've had a major crush on Dylan since middle school. Why didn't you call me and tell me he was up there at camp?"

"Well, for one thing, my cell phone had no connectivity. And besides that, you were teaching Vacation Bible School for all of August, remember?"

"Ugh, don't remind me." She frowned. "Now why exactly did I agree to do VBS in the first place? Especially when I could've been up at Calderwood earning some real money and spending time with dreamy Dylan Morris?"

"Uh . . . you mean besides the fact that your dad's head pastor of our church and your mom is in charge of the kids' ministry and you basically had no choice in the matter?"

"Right . . ." Then Carrie Anne brightened. "So did you talk to him at all? I mean, did you mention me to him or anything?"

Sophie shrugged again.

"Come on, did you?"

"Yeah . . . I talked to him."

"About me?" Carrie's brown eyes were wide and eager.

"I guess . . . your name probably came up."

"And?"

"And, I don't know . . . we talked about a bunch of stuff."

"A *bunch* of stuff?"

Sophie knew she needed to change the subject. "So, are you ever going to finish your lunch? I mean, I still have a lot of shopping to do, and you're just sitting there blabbing on and on and not even touching your food and—"

"Sorry," Carrie Anne snapped. "Excuse me for keeping you waiting."

Sophie snatched up a couple of Carrie Anne's Mexi fries and shoved them in her mouth. "Well, you're the one who's freaking that I'll show up at school wearing something the dog dragged in, or maybe more like something the cat barfed up."

Carrie Anne laughed so hard she snorted.

"Very attractive."

Soon they were back to shopping again. As torturous as it was trying on jeans and tops and skirts and sweaters, it was highly preferable to talking about Dylan Morris. And even though it meant taking fashion advice and some even more ridiculous dieting suggestions from Carrie Anne, as well as purchasing a couple of items that Sophie didn't really like, she knew it was worth the sacrifice to keep any and all questions about the past month and Camp Calderwood and Dylan Morris at bay.

Now all Sophie needed to do was to come up with a viable excuse for not going out to the lake with Carrie Anne on Monday.

2

Of course, by the time Monday came, Carrie Anne would not take no for an answer. "I know you're home alone today, Sophie. And I can tell by the sound of your voice that you're kinda bummed. So get your swimsuit and junk together, because I *will* be picking you up in ten minutes. Be ready or be spaghetti."

Sophie faked a laugh at the worn-out joke. But as soon as she hung up, she felt like screaming . . . or crying. Why hadn't she simply said, "No way, forget it, I am not going"? Or why didn't she just call Carrie Anne back and tell her she was having her period and bad cramps and couldn't possibly do the lake thing today—end of conversation. Sure, it was a lie, but desperate times called for desperate measures.

Instead Sophie ran around her cluttered room gathering up her swimsuit, sunscreen, and sunglasses, all the while reassuring herself that it was entirely possible that Dylan wouldn't be up there anyway. In all likelihood, he'd probably gone off to college by now. After all, Sophie's own brother, Bart, was on his way to campus—in fact, her mom was probably just pulling up to Bart's dorm now. Too bad Sophie had decided not to go on the road trip with them.

Sophie sighed as she stuffed a faded beach towel into her oversized bag. She had considered talking to Bart. She'd imagined herself spilling the beans to him, telling him all about Dylan Morris and how things had gone at Camp Calderwood, and how she was confused about so much and how she had no one to talk to. She knew that her brother, more than anyone else in her family, would have some solid advice for her. Bart, like her, was a strong and committed Christian. He lived his life according to God's Word and was considering going into some form of ministry. Not only that, but it was Bart who had helped Sophie find God back in sixth grade. And it was Bart who would have the right kind of answers now.

But when her brother came home for a short break last week after three weeks of grueling football training, when she finally peeled him away from their dad who only wanted to talk sports, and when the two of them were alone getting ice cream and she finally had the chance to talk to him, she froze up. All she could think was how disappointed he would be in her. She just couldn't bear to see that kind of look in his eyes. So she had made small talk with him and made him laugh. And now he was gone.

"Come on, Sophie!" Carrie Anne yelled. As usual, she'd let herself into the house and was already coming up the stairs. "We're burning daylight here!"

"Coming." Sophie grabbed up her bag and hurried out to see Carrie Anne waiting for her halfway up the stairs. Sophie actually considered faking a fall and pretending to sprain her ankle. But with her luck, she might actually stumble for real and break something or even injure Carrie Anne in the process. Besides, she reminded herself, Dylan was probably on his way to college by now. It was time to just chill.

Carrie Anne grinned as she adjusted the top of her lime green swimsuit. Sophie knew it was her favorite suit—it made her look bigger on top—and she usually reserved it for "special" occasions. All of this did not bode well. Still, Sophie wasn't going there.

"Let's go, girlfriend!" Carrie Anne said.

"Sorry to keep you waiting." Sophie made a face. "What's the rush anyway?"

"The rush is, let's get there already."

Carrie Anne was driving her dad's red Jeep Wrangler today. She had the top down and her straw cowboy hat handy. "Ready to rock and roll?"

"How'd you get so lucky?" Sophie asked as she got in and buckled up.

"Oh, you know. I just batted my big brown eyes and told Dad that he was the best dad in the whole wide world."

"You are such a daddy's girl."

Carrie Anne grinned and put the Jeep in reverse. "And so far, it's working for me."

And you sure know how to work it, Sophie wanted to add, but she knew that sounded rude and a little bit jealous too.

The truth was, Sophie did envy Carrie Anne sometimes, but she'd never admit it to anyone. Except to God, and lately she wasn't even too sure about that. Still, it wasn't always easy being best friends with the pastor's daughter. Not because Pastor Vincent watched every step they took or acted like Big Brother or anything weird or controlling like that. The hardest part was that Carrie Anne's family was so normal, so happy, so nicely connected. They actually had family devotions before dinner every evening. Well, any night when they were all gathered around the table together. And even if it was only half the time, it was twice as often as Sophie's family. Meaning that Sophie's family ate dinner together only on holidays, on birthdays, or by accident.

"Why are you being so quiet?" Carrie Anne turned onto the road that led to the lake.

"Just thinking."

"Can you believe school starts tomorrow?" Carrie Anne groaned loudly. "And don't tell me you're happy about it or I'll puke."

It was a well-established fact that Carrie Anne tolerated school whereas Sophie actually loved it. "It *is* our senior year," Sophie reminded her. "Something we've been looking forward to for like forever. I'd think you'd be glad too."

"Well, I'm sort of okay about that part, except that now all my parents are talking about is college. Make that *arguing.*"

"Arguing?" Sophie couldn't imagine Carrie Anne's parents arguing about anything.

"Yeah, that's probably an overstatement. Mom wants me to live at home and go to the community college." She laughed. "Actually, she thinks I'll be lucky to get in there. But Dad wants me to go to his alma mater."

"Bible college?"

"Yeah." Carrie Anne frowned.

"What do you want?"

"Freedom!" She threw her head back and let out a whoop.

"Meaning you don't want to go to college at all?"

"Meaning I don't want to think about it right now. But Mom's probably right. I should probably go to community college. My grade-point average isn't exactly stellar."

Sophie knew that was an understatement.

"But Dad keeps acting like he's going to pull some strings for Bible college." Carrie Anne glanced nervously at Sophie. "In fact, he's been mentioning you. He's pretty sure you can get a scholarship there."

"Seriously?"

"Yeah. You make me so jealous sometimes. You've always been such a little brainiac."

"You could work harder to get your grades up, Carrie Anne."

"That's what Dad keeps telling me. He was trying to moti-vate me with the idea that we could be roommates in college, like it's going to be so fun and great. I think he plans to have a little talk with you soon."

Sophie blinked. "A talk? With me?"

"You know, to encourage you to help me get my grades up, to take my education seriously. You're the good influence, remember?"

Sophie turned away from Carrie Anne, biting her lip as she watched the pine trees zip past, blending into a blur of green.

"So, anyway, don't act too shocked if Dad asks you to take me by the hand and lead me to the college promised land." Suddenly Carrie Anne was singing that last line, belting it out like she thought she was the next Miley Cyrus or something.

Sophie couldn't help but laugh. "Maybe you should skip college and head straight to Nashville."

"I am rather musical, don'tcha think?"

"That depends on how you define musical."

"I define musical as *Dylan Morris*." Carrie Anne pretended to swoon. "So did he perform at camp? Did you ever hear him sing?"

Sophie coughed. "I think I just swallowed a bug."

"Nasty!" Carrie Anne made a face. "I have gum in my bag."

Sophie grabbed the bag and focused her attention on fishing out a rumpled pack of gum.

"So, did he?"

"Huh?" Sophie shoved a piece of fruit-flavored gum in her mouth and frowned. "What?"

"Did Dylan perform at Camp Calderwood?"

"Oh." Sophie nodded. "Yeah. He was part of the worship team. And he did a few solos too."

"So was he dreamy or not?"

Sophie just shrugged again. She realized she'd been shrugging a lot the past few days. Especially whenever Carrie Anne mentioned Dylan. She needed to be more careful.

"You've been acting so weird lately, Sophie." Carrie Anne glanced her way. "You sure you're okay?"

Sophie thought for a long moment. "No, actually, I'm not okay."

"What?" Carrie Anne looked a little worried.

"I've been meaning to tell you something . . ." Sophie sighed. "You see, the mother ship landed in my backyard last week, and three purple aliens pulled me out of bed and took me aboard and—"

"Very funny." Carrie Anne scowled. "I was trying to be serious."

"Well, then don't."

"Why not?"

"Because . . . ," Sophie threw her head back and let out a loud whoop just like Carrie Anne's, ". . . this is our last day of freedom, and I think we should enjoy it!"

"*Woo-hoo!*" Carrie Anne nodded, then reached down and turned on the radio, which was tuned to the oldies rock station, her dad's favorite. She cranked it up, and the two of them rocked out as she drove down the gravel road toward the lake.

At least Sophie pretended to be rocking out. It was easier than having a real conversation . . . and much easier than talking about Dylan. And it was better than totally freaking over whether or not he'd be at the lake. Although the truth was, she *was* freaking. What would she say to him if he was there? How would she act toward him? Nonchalant and slightly oblivious? Casually friendly but somewhat distant? Downright chilly and cold?

Dylan had promised to call her when they got back home from camp. But he hadn't called. Not once. And she'd checked both the landline at home and her cell—numerous times. It was obvious that he'd forgotten all about her. That he didn't really care. That what they'd had meant nothing to him. And that hurt. A lot.

If Carrie Anne didn't still have such a ridiculous crush on Dylan, Sophie would talk to her about this whole thing. But as it was, Sophie didn't dare mention a thing. She couldn't imagine how Carrie Anne would react. In fact, she didn't want to know. Maybe it was a relief that Dylan was dumping her after all—make that he'd *already* dumped her but just hadn't bothered to send her the memo. Oh, why had she come up here today?

"It looks busy up here," Carrie Anne said as she turned into the first parking area. "Good thing Dylan and his folks came up last week."

"Last week?" Sophie's voice came out sounding like a mouse squeak.

"Yeah. The Morrises have been camping up here for about a week. My mom said it was kind of their last family thing before Dylan heads off to college."

Sophie felt a sudden jolt of hope. "Do cell phones work up here?"

Carrie Anne shrugged as she snagged a skinny parking spot, neatly wedging the Jeep between an SUV and a tree trunk. "I don't know. Do you need to call someone?"

Sophie smiled faintly. "Not really . . . I just wondered." She grabbed up her bag, digging around until she found her lip gloss and a hairbrush.

"Primping?" Carrie Anne peered curiously at Sophie.

Sophie felt her cheeks grow warm. "Hey, you're the one who's always nagging me to care about my appearance."

Carrie Anne chuckled. "And I always figured when that happened, I'd start to care about my grades."

"Maybe we're changing places, kind of like that old movie—*Freaky Friday.*"

"No way." Carrie Anne pulled out her makeup pouch. Tilting the rearview mirror her direction, she quickly made sure she was looking good. "I'm not ready to trade in my looks for brains just yet."

Sophie tried not to take that as an insult, but as they got out of the car, she knew what Carrie Anne meant. She wasn't being mean, just honest. And really, Sophie told herself, wouldn't she rather be smart than beautiful? Wasn't that one of the very things that Dylan had said attracted him to her in the first place? Her mind? Her spirit? And her commitment to God?

Sophie pulled out her cell phone as they walked down the grassy slope toward the dock area. No connectivity. So . . . what if all this time Dylan had really *wanted* to call her but just couldn't use his cell phone out here? What if she'd blown this whole thing out of proportion for nothing? Poor Dylan had been stuck out here at the lake, and she'd been stuck in town—separated by their families and by the lack of cell phone service. Kind of like Romeo and Juliet. Okay, not quite that dramatic, but it sounded good. Anyway, it was entirely possible that Dylan was sitting down there on the dock right now, pining away and just waiting for her to make her appearance and to make his day.

She imagined Dylan's long-limbed gait as he galloped up the hill toward her, his shaggy brown hair ruffled in the wind, his bright smile framed in his handsome, tanned face. He would lean down and swoop her into his arms. He would look directly into her eyes and tell her how much he had missed her. And then they would kiss—

"Earth to Sophie!"

"Huh?"

"I was just saying that looks like the Morris boat over there." Carrie Anne was pointing to a canary yellow ski boat pulling what looked like a wakeboard rider. "And I'll bet that's Dylan in back."

Sophie squinted behind her sunglasses, peering out over the shiny blue lake to where a lanky guy was doing a jump over the wave being made by the boat's wake. She nodded. "I think you're right."

"And there's Dad at the dock," Carrie Anne said. She grabbed Sophie's hand and began to run. "Let's hurry before he takes off again."

Sophie did a pretty decent job of keeping up with Carrie Anne's longer legs, and the truth was that she was anxious to get down to the water too. They had just reached the boat ramp area when one of her flip-flops decided to flop instead of flip, and the next thing she knew, she was facedown in the gravel.

"Oh, Sophie!" Carrie Anne cried. "Are you okay?"

Sophie reached up for Carrie Anne's extended hand, letting her friend help pull her back to her feet. "I, uh, I think so."

"Oh no!" Carrie Anne looked worried. "Your chin is bleeding."

Sophie reached for her chin, which was throbbing like someone had just smacked it with a sledgehammer.

"And your arms—and your legs!" Carrie Anne's eyes were huge. "You look like hamburger—raw hamburger."

"Thanks a lot."

"Sorry." Carrie Anne gently led Sophie toward the day camp area.

"Oh, Sophie," Mrs. Vincent called as she hurried over to meet them. "What happened?"

"She fell down in the gravel," Carrie Anne said.

"Oh dear." Mrs. Vincent frowned. "There's a first-aid kit in the boat. Run and get it, Carrie Anne."

The next thing Sophie knew, she was sitting on a wooden bench, feeling like she was about six years old, and Mrs. Vincent was carefully extracting pieces of gravel from her knees and elbows and chin. Soon she was cleaning the wounds and then applying some kind of greasy ointment. To make matters worse, several friends of the Vincents were now gathered about to watch the spectacle.

"Wow, that looks like it hurts," Mrs. Stewart said. Sophie forced a smile for her as she picked a piece of gravel from her elbow. She didn't know the Stewarts too well, except that Mr. Stewart had attended seminary with Carrie Anne's dad and maybe Dylan's as well.

"Your chin is starting to look like Jay Leno's." This from a blonde girl in a turquoise bikini. Sophie suspected she might be the Stewarts' youngest daughter, but the girl had sure grown up since the last time Sophie had seen her.

"April Lynnette!" Mrs. Stewart scolded.

April just laughed. "Sorry, Mom, but it's the truth."

Sophie's hand was on her chin, partly to hide it and partly to determine whether or not it was fractured. Was it possible to break your chinbone?

Finally, like putting the cherry on top, Mrs. Vincent plastered Sophie's wounds with brightly colored bandages. "Sorry about the Disney theme," she told Sophie. "But it's the only way I can get the boys to allow me to put a bandage on them these days."

"What's up?" a familiar male voice asked from behind the small crowd of onlookers.

"Hey, Dylan," April said. "Nice ride out there."

"Thanks. But what's going—" He stopped suddenly, looking straight into Sophie's face and then quickly away.

"Sophie had a little accident," Carrie Anne explained. She smiled shyly, almost hopefully, at Dylan.

Sophie wanted to die. Instead she looked down at her thighs, which suddenly seemed larger than life, splayed out like filets on the hard wooden bench. If only she could just vanish—*poof*. *Beam me up, Scotty*.

"You should've seen her," April said with macabre enthusiasm. "Running down the boat ramp, and then *splat*—she fell smack on her face. Don't you think her chin looks kinda like Jay Leno's?"

"April!"

"Sorry." April giggled.

Sophie looked up to see that April had her arm linked with Dylan's. She was smiling up at him like they had just said their vows and were ready to head out for their honeymoon. "I want to go out in your boat now, Dylan. Will you teach me to do that jump like you said you would?"

Dylan looked at Sophie again. His eyes looked sad . . . and something else too. Maybe just worried, like he was afraid she was going to say something—something that might blow his cover.

"Come on," April said. "Are you going to teach me or what?"

"Uh, yeah, I guess so," he said to her. He turned back to Sophie. "I hope you're going to be okay."

She forced a smile and held up a brightly bandaged arm. "Yeah, and when Mrs. Vincent is done, I think I'll join the circus."

They all laughed. Dylan, seemingly satisfied that Sophie wasn't going to do or say anything embarrassing, turned and walked back toward the dock. April was still clinging to him, and Sophie thought she could see the bounce return to his steps as he got farther away from her. Soon the others dispersed too, going their separate ways. Dads and kids down to the boats, the other moms back to the picnic site. Sophie encouraged Carrie Anne to go out in the boat with her dad and her little brothers.

"But what about you? Aren't you coming?"

Sophie shook her head, smiling as big as she could manage and hoping to fend off tears. "No, I think I better stay out of the water today."

"I think that's wise, Sophie," Mrs. Vincent said. "You don't want to risk getting an infection."

Soon the boats were loaded up and roaring away from the dock. Mrs. Vincent led Sophie over to join the middle-aged moms. To make matters worse, Sophie suddenly found herself alone with Dylan's mom. Mrs. Vincent had just introduced them before she and Mrs. Stewart headed over to the pump for a bucket of dishwashing water.

"That was quite a fall," Mrs. Morris said.

Sophie smoothed down the edge of a pink Minnie Mouse bandage on her right forearm and nodded. "I know. It's like one minute you're having a good time, and the next thing you know, you're a limping, walking billboard for the Disney channel."

Mrs. Morris chuckled. "At least you've got a sense of humor about it."

"Yeah . . . sometimes that's all a girl's got."

3

Sophie swatted a mosquito on her neck and imagined herself not only bruised and scabby for the first day back at school, but swollen with insect bites as well. Lovely.

Still longing to disappear, she quietly moved her chair a few feet away from the middle-aged mom club and settled into the tree shadows, where she proceeded to sip a Diet Coke and daydream about what it would be like to attend her own funeral. Hopefully Dylan would come . . . and feel guilty.

Soon the moms, not even noticing her, were chatting candidly among themselves. They seemed perfectly oblivious to the fact that Sophie was still sitting nearby and listening. She considered warning them that a spy was in their midst, and then decided, *Why bother?*

"So how are you feeling about Dylan leaving home for college?" Mrs. Vincent asked. "Empty-nest syndrome hitting you yet?"

"Not quite. But I'll admit it's not easy to see your only child leave home." Mrs. Morris frowned. "And I know you've heard some of the PK horror stories."

"PK horror stories?" Mrs. Stewart looked confused.

Mrs. Vincent sighed. "Surely you've heard tales about how pastors' kids go bonkers in college. How they rebel and party and drink and all that sort of nonsense. But I think it's highly exaggerated."

"Maybe so, but I can't deny that it worries me sometimes."

"Oh, kids will be kids," Mrs. Stewart said. "They all need to rebel a little bit. That's how they grow up."

"That's easy for you to say," Mrs. Morris said. "You're not a pastor's wife anymore."

"Well, I still remember what it's like," Mrs. Stewart said. "The only difference between pastoring and lawyering is you get to bill your clients." She chuckled.

"Even so," Mrs. Vincent continued, "there's a lot of pressure on families in the ministry. We need to be perfect . . . Our kids need to be perfect."

Mrs. Stewart nodded. "I suppose that's true. Maybe being married to a workaholic attorney has its upside after all."

They continued to chat among themselves, and for the most part Sophie managed to tune them out. But she couldn't help but wonder about what Dylan's mom had just insinuated. She seemed genuinely worried about her son, about the fact that he might make some wrong choices. Well, maybe she should be worried. Dylan might claim to be a strong Christian, but he certainly wasn't an angel. The way he had treated Sophie wasn't anything to be proud of. Not that Sophie wanted to think about that now.

Suddenly her ears perked up again.

"That Dylan's *always* been the lady killer," Mrs. Vincent was saying. "Even when he was a toddler, he had those thick, long lashes and that million-dollar smile. I can still remember how he could coax me into an extra cookie after you'd told him he'd had enough already."

Mrs. Morris laughed. "That's our Dylan. Always the charmer."

"And always a string of girls trailing after him."

"Don't I know it." Mrs. Morris shook her head. "His dad and I have warned him over and over, the boy needs to keep his guard up when it comes to the girls. Good grief, some of them just throw themselves at him. We keep telling him to stay strong in his convictions and to honor his commitments. But it's not easy for a young man."

"And there's my April, doing just what you said—she's practically throwing herself at the poor boy." Mrs. Stewart chuckled. "I swear, she just got that swimsuit and suddenly she thinks she's all that and a bag of chips."

Mrs. Morris just smiled. "Oh, April doesn't worry me so much. I think Dylan respects that she's only fifteen. And he's always treated her like a little sister. I doubt that's going to change now."

"That's what Carrie Anne says about Dylan too." Mrs. Vincent laughed. "Not that she appreciates being treated like a little sister that much."

Sophie cleared her throat and slowly stood up.

"Oh, I'm sorry, dear," Mrs. Vincent said. "I almost forgot you were still here. I'll bet our conversation is making you uncomfortable."

"Or putting you to sleep," Mrs. Morris added.

"Are you feeling okay, Sophie?" Mrs. Vincent peered up at her. "You look a little pale."

"I'm just kind of stiff and sore. I wish I'd driven out here myself, then I could go home and—"

"I know—why don't you just take the Jeep and drive yourself home?" Mrs. Vincent suggested.

"But wouldn't Pastor Vincent be—"

"Nonsense." Mrs. Vincent was already reaching for her purse. "I have my own set of keys." She handled them like a prize. "And you're a better driver than Carrie Anne is anyway."

Mrs. Morris chuckled. "That's not saying a lot. Hasn't Carrie Anne been in several wrecks since she got her license?"

"They weren't all her fault," Sophie said.

"Anyway, Sophie has a much safer driving record." Mrs. Vincent handed Sophie the keys and patted her hand. "She's also got a much better *academic* record." She smiled sadly. "I just wish you could rub off onto my daughter a bit more, Sophie."

"You're sure it's okay to take the Jeep?" Sophie clutched the keys. She so wanted out of here.

"Of course. Just drive carefully. I'll drop Carrie Anne off at your house later to pick up the Jeep. Now you just go home, take some Advil, and get some rest."

"And put some ice on that chin," Mrs. Morris called out.

Sophie thanked them and moved as quickly as she could toward the parking lot. All she wanted was to escape from those mothers and their aggravating conversation. And away from the others before the boats came back and they returned to camp for lunch and to gape at Sophie like she was a side-show freak.

But mostly she just wanted to escape from Dylan. She could tell—by the way he had looked at her (or rather, the way he hadn't looked at her), by the way he had spoken to her (or avoided speaking), and by the way he couldn't wait to get away from her—that it really was over. Almost as if it had never been. What they'd had was finished, and it was meant to be buried and forgotten. Sophie was no fool. She should've known that this was how it would end.

She cautiously backed up the Jeep, thankful that her brother had taught her how to drive a clutch when she was only fifteen. She took care not to scrape against the tree trunk or the bulky SUV. How had Carrie Anne managed to wedge the Jeep there so tightly?

Finally out of harm's way and exiting the parking lot, Sophie took in a long, deep breath. She asked herself how an intelligent girl like her had ever fallen for someone like Dylan in the first place. Why hadn't she known better? How could someone so smart do something so freaking stupid?

"It's easy," he had told her on that first day they'd spent time together at camp. It was matinee Wednesday, and while the prepubescent campers were parked in front of a full-length film with unlimited junk food, the camp counselors got to enjoy a little break—two blessed hours free from all responsibilities.

"I'm really, really scared." Sophie stood there, frozen with fear, staring at the big log that stretched like a bridge over a fast-moving creek about twenty feet below.

"Come on," Dylan urged her. "You can do it."

"No, I can't," she said. "I have absolutely no sense of balance."

"Just hold my hand." He calmly extended his hand to her, smiling that gorgeous smile. Without even thinking, she took it. And perhaps for the first time ever—or at least for as long as her seventeen-year-old memory served—Sophie's body slipped into motion, moving effortlessly and almost unconsciously, following his lead. It was almost as if they were dancing. Her steps matched his, and like a dream, she gracefully made her way across the log. It was truly magical.

Of course, she had to go and lose it on the other side. She shrieked as her foot slipped on a piece of damp moss, and she knew she was history. She envisioned herself splattered down below—rescuers struggling to pluck her lifeless body from the creek, the camp director calling her parents and informing them of the sad news.

But in that very same instant, Dylan reached out and grabbed her hands with both of his and pulled her toward him onto solid ground. "Careful there," he warned.

Her heart pounded like a jackhammer as he continued to hold on to both her hands, steadying her and gently edging her away from harm's way and toward him. Finally they stood face-to-face. She was just inches from him, and her hands, still clasping his, were now shaking uncontrollably. Whether it was from fear or unbridled passion, she wasn't even sure. But when he looked down into her eyes, she knew she didn't care. His eyes were an intense blue, like a deep mountain lake. She imagined herself diving into that lake and swimming.

"See?" His face came closer to hers. So close she could feel his warm breath. "I knew you could do it, Sophie." And then, like a dream come true, he kissed her . . .

Suddenly a horn honked from behind the Jeep, and Sophie realized now that the light had already turned green. She put the Jeep into first and too quickly released the clutch, causing the engine to stall. Bart's words echoed in her head: "Don't pop the clutch, Sophie. Nice and easy." The horn behind her blasted again—three times—like maybe she couldn't hear it.

Pressing her lips tightly together, she stepped on the clutch and restarted the ignition, taking off more slowly, more carefully this time. "Get a life," she muttered as she made her way across the intersection. But even as she said it, she knew she was talking to herself as much as to the impatient driver behind her. Seriously, it was time for her not only to get a life but to get a grip, and to just get over it. The sooner the better. That is, unless she wanted to drown in sorrow and guilt, like she'd been doing for more than a week now.

"Dear God," she began to pray aloud as she turned down the street to her house. "I am so sorry. Okay? I am really, truly, seriously sorry. Please, please forgive me. Please help me to start over again. I really, really need you now, God. And I'm really, really sorry." She parked the Jeep in front of her house, turned off the engine, leaned her head on the steering wheel, and whispered, "I'm so very, very sorry, God. Amen."

It was the first time she'd genuinely prayed in more than three weeks—ever since she'd first fallen for Dylan. She just hoped that God understood the reason for this little lapse in communication. She hoped that he was as kind and gracious and forgiving as she had once believed him to be. And she hoped that, as Pastor Vincent liked to say, God was capable of do-overs.

Because right now, more than anything else, Sophie needed a fresh start.

4

"Ew, Sophie!" Kelsey North looked up from her lunch with a sickened expression. "What happened to you?"

"I was run over by a truck." Sophie sat down and glared across the table at Kelsey. "What does it look like?"

"Seriously?" This came from Jenny Garcia.

"Give her a break," Carrie Anne said. "She tripped and fell, okay?"

"I thought maybe you just had a huge zit on your chin." Hannah Johnston smiled so big that her teeth looked straighter and whiter than usual against her bronze complexion.

"Funny." Sophie stuck a straw in her soda and wished for teeth as nice as Hannah's . . . and for this day to end. The first day back at school and all her friends were obsessed with how horrible she looked. Why couldn't they just get over it?

"So, long time no see, Sophie." Jenny leaned forward. "Tell us, what did you do on your summer vacation?"

"Yeah," Kelsey said. "I heard you were a counselor at middle school camp. Did you like lose your mind or something?"

These girls were friends from youth group, but it was the first time Sophie had seen any of them since early in the summer. Somehow she'd gotten the mistaken idea she'd missed them.

"Hey, I heard that Dylan Morris was at that same camp," Jenny said.

"He was," Carrie Anne said.

"You got to spend a whole month in the same camp as dreamy Dylan?" Kelsey looked suitably impressed.

Jenny just laughed. "Like it would matter."

"What's that supposed to mean?" Sophie demanded.

"Oh, you know . . ." Jenny got more serious. "It's not like you and Dylan would, you know, start dating or anything like that."

"But they *did* talk," Carrie Anne pointed out. "Right, Sophie? You said you guys talked."

Sophie just rolled her eyes and pretended to be totally absorbed in opening a packet of ketchup and slowly squeezing it out onto her fries. Fries that Carrie Anne had already warned her against. Not that Sophie cared as she ate one after another.

"Yeah, well, talking is just talking," Jenny said. "Now, if I had my chance, I'd do way more than just talk to someone like Dylan Morris."

"Like you'd ever get the chance." Carrie Anne's voice sounded a little sharp. "Dylan wouldn't give a girl like you a second glance."

Hannah gave Carrie Anne a nudge with her elbow, like she was warning her not to go there. Sophie had to agree, but she wasn't going to say anything.

"Meaning?" Jenny looked genuinely offended.

"I know what she means," Kelsey said quietly.

Jenny made a bored expression. "Fine, let me guess. You're going to start lecturing me about taking the purity pledge again, right?"

Of their group of Christian friends, Jenny was the only one who had refused to take the pledge a few years ago—to promise to abstain from sex until marriage. Jenny had claimed the pledge was hypocritical. Although Sophie hadn't got that back then. She'd figured it was simply Jenny's excuse to blow it. Not that she had. At least not that Sophie had ever heard about.

"For your information," Carrie Anne said, "there are certain guys—the kind of guys who are *worth* waiting for—who appreciate the kind of girls who've made that pledge."

"Yeah, whatever." Jenny just shrugged.

"And Dylan Morris happens to be one of them," Kelsey finished for her.

"Right, Sophie?" Carrie Anne looked at her.

Sophie just nodded, but suddenly she wasn't hungry anymore. In fact, she felt all hot and prickly, and kind of like she'd just stepped off a Tilt-a-Whirl ride, only worse. She stood up and grabbed her bag.

"What's wrong?" Hannah looked up with a frown.

"I'm done." Sophie stepped back.

"Are you okay?" Carrie Anne asked.

"Yeah, you look like—"

But Sophie was already leaving—heading straight to the girls' restroom. She barely made it to the first stall, and suddenly she was hurling into the toilet. She barfed so hard it felt like her brains were coming out. Finally she stopped and slowly stood up. Her head was throbbing, her heart was pounding, and all she wanted was to just lie down . . . and die.

"I told you those fries are lethal." Carrie Anne pushed open the door behind her. "Gross!"

Without looking at her, Sophie flushed the toilet. Then she pulled off some toilet paper and used it to wipe her mouth and wipe the sweat off her face.

"Are you going to be okay?" Carrie Anne called from the sink area. "Ya want me to call for the school nurse or something?"

Sophie stepped out of the stall and slowly walked over to the sink. But she just stood there staring into the mirror. A scrap of white toilet paper was hanging from the ugly scab on her chin. "I'm a mess."

"I'll say." Carrie Anne gently peeled the toilet paper from Sophie's chin.

Sophie stepped onto the foot pedal that turned on the water, then dipped her hands into the spray, tossing some of it onto her face.

"Do you think it's the flu?" Carrie Anne asked as she handed Sophie a couple of paper towels then quickly stepped back. "Excuse me if I don't get too close."

Sophie blotted her face with the paper towels. Tears were threatening again. She pushed the cool, damp paper on her closed eyes, telling herself not to start crying. She'd already made a spectacle of herself. Enough was enough already.

"I think you should go see the school nurse," Carrie Anne said with conviction. "You might be really sick. Maybe it's from falling down yesterday."

"Like falling-down sickness?" Sophie crumpled the towels, tossed them into the trash, and forced a smile.

Carrie Anne snickered as she handed Sophie her purse. "At least you're still funny."

Sophie put the strap of her bag over her shoulder and sighed.

"But I still think you should see the school nurse. I'll walk you there, okay?"

Sophie just shook her head. "No, go back to your lunch."

"What about you? And your lunch?"

Sophie nodded toward the stall. "I left it in there."

"But what if you're contagious?"

Sophie considered this. "Fine, if it makes you feel better, I'll go see the nurse. Just go back and finish your lunch, okay?"

"Okay . . ."

"And don't tell Jenny and Kelsey and Hannah."

"What?"

"That I just lost my cookies in here."

Carrie Anne smiled impishly. "And I so wanted to tell Jenny that she'd made you sick."

Sophie walked slowly toward the school office. She really had no desire to see the school nurse today. The last time she'd seen a school nurse was in fourth grade, right after she'd fallen from the monkey bars and split open her chin. Sophie had been bleeding so profusely that the nurse had looked like she was about to faint before she had the good sense to place a towel on Sophie's chin and tell her to "apply pressure."

Sophie reached up to see if she could feel where she'd eventually gotten six stitches, right below her jawline, but her chin was still so swollen from yesterday's fall that she couldn't even feel the scar. She was such a klutz.

"The nurse is at lunch," the receptionist told Sophie. And this after Sophie had given her full name and that she might have the flu.

"Okay." Sophie started to leave.

"But she should be back in a few minutes."

Sophie studied the gray-haired woman. She had kind eyes and nodded over to what appeared to be a fairly comfortable-looking tweed sofa. "Why don't you sit down and wait?"

"Thanks." Sophie went over and flopped down on the sofa. Leaning back, she closed her eyes and imagined she was home and in her room, still sleeping in bed, and this day hadn't yet begun. Better yet, she was home and in her room, sleeping in bed, and it was still July and she hadn't gotten her heart broken by Dylan Morris yet. Oh yeah, the good old days.

"The nurse will see you now," a quiet voice said.

Sophie sat up and blinked into the overhead light, startled to realize that she wasn't at home in bed but was sitting in the school office. She had actually fallen asleep.

"Mrs. Bernard is back from lunch," the receptionist said. "She's in her office now."

"Oh yeah." Sophie stood up, vaguely wondering if she had drooled in her sleep, or if she had spittle hanging from her scabby chin. She touched it gently and was relieved to discover it seemed to be dry. Still sore, but not coated in slobber.

"Sophie Ramsay." The nurse stuck out her hand and shook Sophie's. "I'm Mrs. Bernard, the school nurse." She pointed to a chair opposite her desk. "Go ahead and take a seat."

"Thanks." Sophie sat down, placed her bag in her lap, and waited.

"Now, what seems to be your problem?" Mrs. Bernard frowned slightly. "Were you in some kind of an accident?"

Sophie quickly explained yesterday's tumble at the lake and then how she'd just hurled in the girls' restroom.

"Goodness, you're having a little bad luck, aren't you?"

"I guess."

"Well, it's a little early for flu season, but you never know." She was getting something out of a cabinet. It turned out to be an electronic thermometer, which she placed on Sophie's forehead. After a few seconds, she said, "Just a little over normal." Then she checked Sophie's throat and eyes. She poked here and there and finally proclaimed her to be healthy. "Maybe it was just something you ate," she told Sophie as she closed the cabinet.

"So, I'm not contagious?"

"Not as far as I can see." Mrs. Bernard peered curiously at Sophie as she folded her arms across her front. "And shall I assume that there's no chance you're pregnant, Sophie?"

Sophie blinked in surprise. "No," she said quickly, "of course not. I mean, I've taken the purity pledge and everything." As soon as she said that, she realized how stupid it sounded. She felt her cheeks flushing, and she just really wanted to get out of there. She stood. "So, I should go back to class now?"

"If you feel well."

"Yeah." Sophie nodded. "I feel fine."

"The receptionist will give you a hall pass."

"Thanks."

"Take care. And if you start to feel worse, just come on back."

Sophie assured the nurse that she would do that, but as she hurried over to the English department with her hall pass in hand, she knew the nurse's office was the last place she wanted to go. She'd had enough of Nurse Bernard and her nosy insinuations.

Carrie Anne caught up with Sophie again after fifth period. "So . . . are you contagious?"

Sophie forced a laugh. "You should be so lucky. If I was contagious, you might've caught some of my intelligence and you wouldn't have to spend a whole day in school, whereas I am now free to go home. Adios, amiga."

"Don't rub it in."

"Sorry." Sophie patted her on the back. "But it is a relief to get out of here."

"Well, you've had kind of a rough day."

"These senior half days seem like a pretty good idea right now."

"Think of me"—Carrie Anne sighed—"while you're out there enjoying your freedom. So, what are you going to do to celebrate? Go to the mall? Pig out on junk food?"

"I'm sure I'll think of something," Sophie assured her. But the truth was that she planned to simply go home and take a nap—to temporarily escape her life and to hopefully not dream about Dylan.

It was surprisingly hot out, and she opened both doors to her Nissan to let some fresh air in before she finally got inside. She heard her stomach rumble and briefly considered Carrie Anne's comment about getting junk food, but the memory of partially digested fries and ketchup floating in the toilet quickly wiped that temptation aside. Instead, she drove straight home. To her pleasant surprise, her mom's car had just pulled into the driveway too. They both got out at the same time.

"Mom!" Sophie cried as she ran across the driveway to give her mom a big hug. "Welcome home."

"Well, that was certainly unexpected." Her mom stepped back, then studied Sophie with a perplexed expression. "What happened to you, sweetie?"

It took Sophie a moment to remember, but then she explained about falling at the lake. She almost told her about barfing at school as well but decided not to overwhelm the poor woman.

Her mother frowned at her watch. "But what're you doing home from school early?"

"Remember senior half days?"

Her mom slapped her forehead. "Oh, I totally forgot."

"If I didn't already have all my AP classes, I'd probably go all day anyway. But as it is, I don't really see the point."

Mom put her arm around Sophie's shoulders. "That's what comes from being such a good student, Sophie. You and your brother make me so proud."

Sophie grinned. "So was Bart glad to get back to campus?"

"I think so. He had to get right to practice, though. You know they have that big game this coming weekend."

Sophie helped her mom with her bags, and they chatted as they went into the house. For a while, Sophie thought this was how it was supposed to be—mom and daughter just hanging together. But it wasn't long before Mom announced she had to go to work.

"But it's after two o'clock," Sophie pointed out.

"I know, but I promised Dolores I'd come in for the three-to-nine shift for the rest of the week in exchange for the time I took off for Bart. It's still the back-to-school season, and Dolores told me they've been crazy busy." Sophie's mom had been working part-time at Staples for several years now, but she usually didn't work later than seven at night.

So once again, Sophie had the whole house to herself. But instead of enjoying the freedom of cranking up her music or making a mess in the kitchen (which she almost always cleaned up afterward) or watching whatever she wanted on Dad's big-screen TV, Sophie just sat in the kitchen and felt lonely. Then she headed for her room. As she trudged up the stairs, she couldn't remember when she'd felt so tired. Or was she just bored? Maybe she was depressed. She just wanted to go to sleep, to escape . . . everything.

5

When Sophie woke up, it was to the sound of an alarm ringing loudly and the smell of acrid smoke. Heart racing and certain that the house was on fire, she leaped from her bed and dashed downstairs.

Smoke was billowing from the kitchen, and on closer investigation, she realized it was simply from the remains of a Hungry Man dinner that appeared to have been torched in the oven. And the cause of the noise was the fire alarm in the laundry room. It had probably already gone off once and then must've detected smoke again for a second. At least the oven was turned off now, but the cook—her dad—was nowhere in sight. She opened windows and turned on the fan and wondered why on earth her dad had decided to heat his dinner in the oven rather than the usual microwave. And, furthermore, why he had taken off without even warning his daughter that she might be about to die from asphyxiation.

Her guess was that he was in a grumpy mood tonight. That he'd come home expecting his wife to be here but she was gone. Not only that, but his teenage daughter was sleeping—lazy girl! And so he'd turned on the oven, shoved in the frozen dinner, and zoned out in front of some sports show, only to be awakened by a fire alarm and smoke. Then he'd probably gotten really mad, used some choice words, jumped into his big diesel Ford pickup, and beat cheeks over to Hank's Diner, where he would order something dripping in fat and complain to the waitress that no one understood him. Or something like that.

Sophie gingerly removed the offensive burnt offering from the oven, carried it out to the metal trash can outside, and dumped it.

"Everything okay in there?" called out Mrs. Poindexter from next door.

Sophie gave the old woman a smile. "I think my dad decided to cremate his dinner tonight."

Mrs. Poindexter made her way slowly across her driveway toward Sophie. "Well, I smelled smoke and heard that ringing noise, and I was about to call the fire department."

"Thanks, but it's under control now. Sorry about the noise."

She nodded, then looked concerned. "Goodness gracious, Sophie girl, what in the world has happened to your face?"

Once again Sophie explained about falling at the lake.

"Oh my, you know what the Good Book says, don't you?"

"What's that?"

"Pride comes before a fall."

Sophie considered this. "So, do you think that's what made me fall?"

"Were you feeling mighty proud of yourself about something?"

Sophie shook her head. "Not even close."

The old woman smiled. "Then I'm sure it wasn't related."

Sophie sighed.

"How old are you now, Sophie girl?"

"Seventeen. But I'll be eighteen in February."

"You're nearly grown then." She shook her head. "You kids grew up so fast. Seems like yesterday you and your brother were playing in the sprinklers, dressing up for trick or treat. And now you're a grown woman."

Sophie laughed. "Well, not really a *grown* woman."

Mrs. Poindexter shook her finger at her. "I was just your age when I wed my Arlen more than seventy-five years ago. And just eighteen when I had my first baby." She chuckled. "Not that I recommend it. No, no . . . the younger generation is smart to wait."

Sophie nodded somberly.

Mrs. Poindexter took Sophie's hand and clasped it warmly. "You are a very smart girl, Sophie. Why, I still remember when you were a little thing, and how you'd come over and play chess with Mr. Poindexter while he was recovering from heart surgery. Do you remember that?"

Sophie nodded again, smiling a bit this time. "He was a good chess player."

"Well, one day after you left, he took me aside and told me that you were the smartest child he'd ever laid eyes on." Her faded eyes lit up. "And if you knew my husband, you knew that was high praise indeed."

Sophie didn't know what to say to that.

"And I know how you thought he was letting you win sometimes, Sophie girl. But the truth is, he never did." Mrs. Poindexter chuckled. "Nope, he never did." She sighed and glanced back at her house. "Well, I better get back before my own fire alarms start going off. I've got green beans cooking." She turned and slowly walked back to her house.

Sophie stood there thinking about what Mrs. Poindexter had just told her. She had no idea that Mr. Poindexter hadn't been *letting* her win. In fact, she distinctly remembered him teasing her, saying that if and when she won, it was simply because he felt sorry for her. Anyway, it was a sweet story and a nice compliment. But she'd been a child then, and despite having a high IQ, she'd been a bit on the naive side. Maybe she still was.

The truth was, she hadn't changed all that much. In the same way she'd fallen for Mr. Poindexter's tricks back then, she'd fallen for Dylan's deception just a few weeks ago. For a smart girl, she was pretty dumb. Or maybe she was just living in denial. Deep, dark denial. And if ignorance was bliss, which seemed unlikely, then knowledge was power.

Sophie marched into the house, grabbed her purse, ran out to her car, and drove to the nearest Walgreen's. She parked the car and hurried inside, heading straight to the feminine hygiene department. She searched until she found what she was looking for—an early pregnancy test.

She glanced over her shoulder to see if anyone was around, then picked up the box and began scanning the back.

"Hurry up," said a girl who was coming her way.

"Just chill," another girl said.

Sophie shoved the box back onto the shelf and turned her attention to the rack next to it. Unfortunately that was the birth control section. As the two girls, both from her school, approached, Sophie reached out and grabbed a package of sanitary pads without looking closely at them. She wasn't a pad user since she preferred tampons, but anything was better than being caught with an at-home pregnancy kit.

Acting as if nothing was unusual, she turned and carried the large, hot pink package of pads to the registers, getting into the line with only one woman in it. As it turned out, the pads she'd chosen were some kind of supersized, mega-absorbent, recommended-for-elephant-use sort of product. And when she got to the cash register, she realized that a guy about her age was the cashier.

Avoiding his eyes, she shoved the enormous package to-ward him, and with heat racing up her neck, she fumbled in her wallet for the right amount of cash. What were the chances of a robbery just then? A masked man could burst into the drugstore and just shoot her. Of course, with her luck, the morning paper would read Teenage Girl Found Dead with Maxi Pads Clasped in Her Arms.

Sophie heard the girls laughing as she made her way out of the store. They were probably just laughing for the sake of laughing. That's what girls her age did. But it sure felt as if they were laughing at her, as if they had known what she'd been up to, as if they could read her like a book.

She threw the detestable Walgreen's bag into the backseat and started her car again. Maybe she should just give up this fool's errand. Maybe being the queen of denial wasn't such a bad thing after all. Maybe her suspicions were totally wrong. Seriously, it wouldn't be the first time she'd been wrong about something, now would it?

She drove across town, considering the possibilities. She could just continue like she'd been doing—telling herself that she was delusional, that no way was she pregnant. Seriously, she'd only done it once . . . okay, twice. But that was only if you counted the first time, which didn't actually even seem like the real thing. Or maybe it was just because it had been so painful.

"I'm sorry," Dylan had told her afterward. "Are you okay?"

She hadn't known what to say, what to do. It was all so awkward, so unexpected and messy. She wasn't totally sure what had happened or how, only that it had hurt *a lot*, and that she had told him to stop. But he hadn't seemed to hear her. Maybe that was her fault. Maybe it was all her fault. Maybe she'd given Dylan the impression that she was that kind of a girl—experienced. Or maybe she'd been like those girls Dylan's mother had been complaining about—the ones who chased him relentlessly. And then she had caught him, even if only temporarily.

Sophie parked in front of a Wal-Mart now. But with a fairly full parking lot and teens milling about, it seemed even riskier than Walgreen's. Plus, there was Staples—and her mom's car— just across the street.

Finally Sophie decided to drive to the next town, just ten minutes away. She would locate a small drugstore, go straight inside, and look around, and if the coast was clear, she would snatch up an E.P.T. box and head straight for the checkout. In and out. Just like that.

As she drove down the freeway, she considered the possibility of buying a pregnancy test online. She was sure that could be done. Except for two major obstacles: (1) the package would be delivered to her house, and who knew how obvious it might look, and (2) she would probably need a credit card to buy it. Besides that, she would have to wait. And now, especially after losing her lunch in the cafeteria today, she wanted to know.

The more she thought about it, the more certain she felt that Dylan had to have been right when he'd assured her afterward that "no one gets pregnant the first time." Okay, that didn't absolve the second time. But Dylan had brought protection that time. Who would've expected that the condom would rip? Or that he'd have only one? Or that she'd even have been in such a position to start with? Really, how had it happened?

"I love you," he'd told her each time he'd held her close. For the first week, they had met whenever they could, sometimes sneaking out of their cabins after the kids had fallen asleep, and all they did was talk and kiss and talk and kiss. By the second week, Dylan's hands were wandering. But she wasn't stopping him.

He had called her "beautiful, intoxicating, lovely, sumptuous." And hook, line, and sinker, she had bit into it. He'd told her she was "the one" and they were meant for each other, meant to be together. She had assumed that he meant forever. Hadn't he said as much?

It was nearly seven when she pulled up to a run-down-looking drugstore on Main Street. Fortunately it was open, but just barely—about half the lights were already turned off.

"We close at seven," a frumpy clerk said to her. "Better make it quick."

"I will," Sophie called back. The store was small, and it didn't take long to find the right section. But there was only one kind of pregnancy kit there, and it looked dusty and old. She wondered if it was even any good.

"Are you coming?" the clerk called.

Sophie grabbed the box and jogged to the checkout.

"Oh." The woman peered over her reading glasses to examine Sophie more closely. Was she going to ask for ID? The woman just shook her head and rang up the kit.

"It's for my older sister," Sophie said, shoving the twenty toward her.

"Yeah, right." The woman cackled as she took the bill and then counted out the change. "Never heard that one before."

Sophie dumped the change into her purse and waited.

"You want a bag?"

Sophie blinked. "Yeah, if you don't mind."

The woman took out a bag, snapped it open, and slid the test into it. As she handed Sophie the bag, she smiled, revealing some seriously yellowed teeth. "Good luck, girlie."

"Thanks," Sophie muttered. She clutched the bag and hurried out of the store. Who did she think she was fooling?

When she got home, both her dad's pickup and her mom's car were in the driveway. She parked on the street and tucked her package into her bag. She wished she'd thought to bring a larger purse. This one looked stuffed full. What if they noticed? What if they asked where she'd been? What if she looked guilty? What if it all hit the fan?

She rehearsed her answers as she slowly walked up to the house. She'd say that she'd gone out for a bite to eat, run into friends, visited awhile, then remembered she had homework and skedaddled for home. She actually planned to use the word *skedaddled* too. Give them something to think about.

But her parents were snuggled up on the sectional in the family room, apparently watching the TV, although it wasn't even turned to ESPN. They barely noticed her come in.

"I'm home," she called out. "Got homework."

"Okay," her mom called back.

"Good night," her dad added. Like maybe that was a hint.

Really, that was fine with her. What she was about to do needed no adult interruptions or distractions. It would be better if they weren't even home, but she couldn't have everything.

Sophie went straight to the bathroom and locked the door. She pulled out the box, opened it, and carefully read and then reread the instructions until she was certain she knew how to do it. She took out the strip, removed the cap, and realized that she could barely "make a stream," which was supposed to last seven seconds. She counted and only made it to six. Why hadn't she thought to drink a couple of glasses of water and just wait? Now she had wasted a strip.

Just the same, she decided to wait the full five minutes, just out of curiosity. She laid the strip on the edge of the bathtub, then sat down on the toilet seat lid. With her eyes on her watch, she waited.

It was the longest five minutes of her life, and she really didn't expect to see any change on the stick—not with only *six* seconds of urine. But when those five minutes finally ticked by, she went over to look at the stick and was stunned to see that it had changed. The stick now had *two stripes.*

Two stripes meant positive—and positive meant pregnant.

She sank to the edge of the tub and wondered if she was about to have a heart attack. It felt like her chest had imploded and she couldn't breathe. Like the bathroom was beginning to spin, or maybe it was tipping sideways. She clung to the sides of the tub, feeling like she was about to slide in and be sucked down the drain. She wished she could go all the way down the drain and just vanish from the face of the planet forever.

Afraid she was about to faint, she dropped her head between her knees and attempted to breathe. If she fainted in the bathroom and crashed to the floor with a loud thud, her parents would dash up and bust down the door. They would find her passed out on the floor with the evidence of the pregnancy test—and the telltale strip showing TWO stripes. *Two stripes!* How could it be?

Finally her heart rate seemed closer to normal, and breathing became slightly easier. Sophie picked up the pregnancy test box and looked more carefully at it. It was kind of faded and old looking. Maybe it really hadn't worked properly. Was it possible that there was a shelf life or some kind of expiration date on a kit like this? Or that it really needed the full seven seconds to work properly? She wanted to try it again but knew that wasn't going to work just yet. So she drank six glasses of water and just waited and waited and waited. But it just wasn't working.

Finally, feeling like a failure—like, how can someone be so dumb as to mess up a simple test like this?—she put everything from the kit back into the bag, not leaving a trace of it behind. She shoved it back into her purse and retreated to her room.

Maybe the test was faulty. Maybe she'd done it wrong. Because whatever those two stripes were trying to shout at her,

Sophie did not want to listen. She couldn't believe it. And until she could do the test correctly or possibly get a new test, she refused to believe it. She would push the skewed test results from her mind and would focus on homework instead. The queen of denial still reigned.

She went online to do some research for a journalism project, but soon she got distracted in researching home pregnancy tests and why they did or did not always work. To her relief, there seemed to be all kinds of reasons that her results truly were inaccurate. It seemed perfectly clear that her pregnancy test had not worked. Plain and simple, it was wrong. As far as she knew, she was NOT pregnant. Most definitely NOT. Really, God wouldn't allow that to happen. He wouldn't do that to her.

Just to be sure, she prayed. She confessed and repented and begged God to forgive her, to wipe her slate clean, to make her new, to give her a fresh start. And she promised that she would never, never, never break her vow to him again. If he wanted, she would become a nun. Okay, she wasn't even Catholic. But she could convert.

6

It was about one in the morning when Sophie woke up with a strong urge to use the bathroom. As she was climbing out of bed, she remembered the pregnancy test. Seven seconds . . . Maybe she should just give it one more try. Hopefully it would work properly now. This time there would be only one stripe showing. And then she could rest easy.

She fumbled in her purse, trying to keep the rustle of the paper bag quiet as she took out the kit and removed a test strip. Then she put the kit back in the bag, shoved it back in her purse, and hurried to the bathroom.

Seven seconds was no problem this time. In fact, she probably could've done several strips. Satisfied with her effort, she set the damp strip on the edge of the bathtub again and then waited. And waited. She wasn't sure if it had really been five minutes, but she decided to sneak a peek.

Two stripes were showing again.

Sophie stuck the telltale stick in the pocket of her T-shirt to deal with later as she flushed the toilet. She returned to her room, climbed back into bed, and cried herself to sleep.

"Wake up, sleepyhead." Her mom was gently shaking her shoulder. "You'll be late for school."

Sophie jerked awake and stared up at her mom. Did she know? Had she found the kit? Was Sophie's nightmare about to turn into a waking reality?

Her mom smiled. "You must've been really tired. Did you know it's ten minutes until eight?"

"No way!" Sophie looked at her clock. "I better get moving."

"I'll go toast you a bagel and you can eat it on your way to school," Mom called as she hurried away.

"Thanks, Mom." Sophie threw back the covers. There, twisted in the sheets, was the stick from last night. The nasty, awful, horrible stick. *What if Mom had seen it?*

Sophie slipped the stick in the bag that was still concealing the test kit. When no one was around to see, she would dump the whole works in a restroom trash can at school—get rid of the evidence. What she would do after that . . . well, she was pretty much clueless.

She quickly dressed, grabbed up her homework things, then dashed downstairs. She snagged the bagel, thanked her mom, and hurried out the door. Maybe she should get up late every morning. It might make life easier if she didn't have to look her mother in the eyes. As for her dad . . . well, he was fairly oblivious to anything that didn't involve sports or tires.

As Sophie drove to school, she decided there was only one way she would be able to make it through this day, and that was to pretend that nothing whatsoever was wrong. She would pretend that she wasn't freaking out or about to have a total nervous breakdown. And if Oscars could be given to teenage girls who were able to delude everyone—including best friends, parents, teachers, neighbors, maybe even God—she would do whatever it took to win one.

By the end of her day, she felt she had succeeded. Joking had always been her best defense against any form of discomfort. Whether it was a mean girl taking a poke at her weight, an idiot boy gaping at her bustline, or a thoughtless teacher making her out to be "teacher's pet," Sophie had learned early on to deflect these situations with humor and wit. She'd realized this was a skill that would carry her through almost anything. Almost.

"Hey, Sophie, are you going to stick around for the yearbook meeting this afternoon?"

Sophie turned around to see Wes Andrews trailing her. She and Wes had been friends since middle school. They'd both been journalism nerds for years now. Last year they'd been on the newspaper staff as well as the yearbook committee.

Sophie frowned. "Maybe not."

"Maybe not?" Wes looked shocked. "Why not?"

She shrugged. "I don't know . . . I guess I'm not really into it."

He came over and dramatically placed his hand on her forehead. "Are you sick or dying or something?"

She pushed his hand away and faked a laugh. "No. I just thought I'd take a break."

"Take a break from yearbook during your senior year? Are you serious?"

Sophie blew air between her lips as she struggled to come up with an acceptable answer or a joke. But neither came.

"Come on, Sophie," he urged. "We need you."

"I don't see why. I mean, if I'm not there, someone else can step in and—"

"No one can take your place, Sophie. You're brilliant."

She smiled. "Thanks, but if I'm not there, someone else can be brilliant." She tweaked his nose. "Maybe even you."

"This is so wrong." Wes grabbed their journalism teacher before he went into the classroom. "Talk some sense into her, Mr. Young."

"Huh?" Mr. Young adjusted his wire-rimmed glasses and turned to look at Sophie and Wes. "What's up?"

"She's abandoning the yearbook."

Mr. Young frowned. "Is that true?"

Sophie just shrugged.

Mr. Young pressed his lips together, then slowly shook his head. "Sophie, Sophie, Sophie . . . have you thought this through carefully? Surely you realize that being on yearbook and the newspaper looks good on your college applications. And that your participation could possibly lead to a, well, some sort of scholarship." He peered closely at her. "Are you willing to risk—" He was cut off by the bell. "Sorry, I have to go. But make sure you think this over carefully, Sophie." Then he hurried into the classroom.

"So?" Wes's brows lifted.

Sophie let out a quiet groan.

"Seriously, what's the problem?" He studied her face as if looking for a clue. Suddenly she remembered what a great reporter Wes was, how he had a nose for news, and how he was an expert at getting to the bottom of a story.

"There's no problem," she said lightly. "I guess I was just daydreaming about possibly having a life. You know, something beyond staring at the computer screen for hours on end, cutting and pasting and all that."

He frowned. "But that is a life. I mean, don't you want to take journalism in college? Don't you plan to work in it after you get your degree? That's what you've always said. When did you change?"

She considered this. "You're right, Wes. And I do still want that. It's just that—"

"I know." He held his pen up in the air like a torch. "You got a boyfriend, didn't you? During summer vacation you went and got yourself a serious boyfriend. Am I right or am I right?"

She shook her head. "No, you're definitely wrong."

But he didn't look convinced.

"What time is the yearbook meeting?" She knew when it was, but it was a good distraction technique.

"Four. Same as always."

"Fine. I'm going to run home and take a nap, and then I'll see you at four."

Wes grinned. "Be there or be square."

She rolled her eyes. "More like be there *and* be square."

"I better get to class before Mr. Young marks me late."

"Just tell him you talked sense into me and I'm sure he'll excuse you."

Wes nodded and hurried into the classroom, closing the door behind him. Sophie just stood there and sighed. It seemed crazy to get involved in yearbook committee. That was a long-term commitment. And who knew where she'd be by the end of the school year?

Yet she knew that to quit those normal activities would only draw attention—raising a red flag that something really was wrong with her. Better to just play the game. Keep up the act. Maybe eventually she would figure a way out of this mess.

In the meantime, she just wanted to sleep. But as she started her car, her cell phone rang. She was tempted to ignore it, but it was her dad. And since he never called her, she was concerned. What if something had happened to Mom or Bart? Or . . . what if her parents had somehow figured things out? What if she'd left some scrap of evidence in the upstairs bathroom? What if someone had spotted her disposing of the pregnancy kit at school? What if they'd run a DNA test and . . . Okay, she knew she was being ridiculous.

"Hey, Dad," she said. "What's up?"

"Hey, Pumpkin," he said in a surprisingly friendly tone. "Can I ask you a huge favor?"

"Sure, what?"

"Well, Marge broke a tooth eating Corn Nuts, so she's got to run into the dentist, and I need someone to watch the front desk for a couple of hours. I remembered you get off of school early now. Would you mind?"

She so wanted to tell him to forget it, but he was being so nice that she just couldn't. "Well, I have yearbook at four and—"

"That's perfect. Marge was sure she'd be back here by four."

"Okay . . ."

"Hurry."

"You want me to speed?"

"'Course not . . . just don't dawdle."

"Dawdle . . . yeah, right, Dad." She told him good-bye and closed her phone. Great. Just what she needed—two hours of breathing stinky tire-rubber fumes.

Her dad knew she didn't like working at the tire store. They'd been over that enough times over the years. Fortunately her mom supported her on this subject. But sometimes when he was in a pinch, like now, she'd help out.

When she got to the tire store, her dad was in the garage repairing a flat tire, and three people were waiting at the counter. The first guy wanted to pay for his tires and get the keys to his car—pronto.

"I already missed an hour of work," he said, like she was personally responsible that his first credit card was just rejected and she had to run a second one. "And believe me, someone's gotta pay the bills."

"Sorry you had to wait," she said in a fake-sounding cheerful tone. She watched as he signed the receipt, then handed him his keys. "Have a nice day, sir."

He just growled "thanks" and hurried out.

"May I help you?" Sophie asked the woman who was next.

"I sure hope so." The woman sighed and ran her hand over a very rotund midsection. "I want to get home before my kids do, and my back is killing me."

"Sorry about that." Sophie couldn't help but stare at the woman's large belly.

"Yeah, I'm due any day now." She leaned her elbows onto the counter. "And my feet are so swollen I can't even get into my shoes." She sort of laughed. "Not that a young girl like you cares about any of that."

Sophie stood up straighter. "So how can I help you?"

"Well, my neighbor just dropped me off, and my car's supposed to be done by now, but I noticed it's still up on that rack thing out in the garage. And I'm just hoping that there's nothing seriously wrong with it. I brought it in for a brake job and—"

"Tell me your name and I'll go and check on it."

"Gansky. Tricia Gansky. It's the red minivan."

Sophie went into the garage and waited for her dad to finish tightening the last lug nut. He handed her the invoice. "This one's on the house."

"So what's up with that red minivan?" she asked. "Is it ready to go?"

"Not even close. The lady thought she just needed new brake pads, but the drums are shot. I tried to call but got her voice mail."

"So what do I tell her?"

He rubbed his chin. "Better let me explain this one. Why don't you send her out here?"

Sophie frowned at the greasy floor. "She's really huge pregnant, Dad. You wouldn't want her to slip or anything."

He nodded. "Good thinking. Tell her I'll meet her in the waiting area."

Sophie returned and gave the woman a halfhearted smile. "My dad wants to talk to you over there." She nodded to the chairs. "Why don't you put your feet up?"

The woman looked worried. "Sounds expensive."

Sophie just shrugged. "I really don't know." She looked to the next customer, an old guy wearing a Dodgers cap. "Next."

He took his time telling her his name and about how he'd just gotten these brand-new tires less than a month ago and this morning he had a flat. "They just don't make tires like they used to," he continued. "But everything's like that. Instead of getting better, things just get worse. I don't understand it."

She handed him the invoice, and he peered at it.

"I don't see the amount."

"It's free." She handed him the keys.

He looked surprised. "Well now."

She pointed to her dad's writing in the description column. "And it looks like you better check your driveway for nails since that seems to be what flattened your tire."

He smiled sheepishly. "Oh, I was doing a little woodworking project out there the other day. That must've been the problem. Well, thank you very much, young lady." He tipped his cap and left.

Sophie glanced over to where her dad was using his hands to explain something to the pregnant woman. Not that it was helping since she was crying and clearly not getting a word he was saying. Finally her dad glanced her way and nodded at her like he wanted her to come over.

"Why don't you get Mrs. Gansky some water, Sophie." He stood and quickly exited into the garage. Her dad had never liked being around women's emotions. He didn't know how to deal with them.

"Here you go." Sophie handed the woman a chilled water bottle and a couple of Kleenexes.

"I don't know what I'm going to do." The woman wiped her eyes. "I only had enough credit on my card to cover a basic brake job. And now I have to replace the whole works and it's more than three times as much."

"Sorry." Sophie didn't know what else to say.

"And my husband—he got laid off last spring, and we—we don't even have medical insurance." She was sobbing again. "And we've—we've got doctor bills and we'll have hospital bills and now—now this." She loudly blew her nose. "I don't know what we'll do and—"

"Anyone working this counter here?" a middle-aged man called out.

"I'm coming." Sophie patted the woman's shoulder. "I'm sure it looks worse than it is."

The woman looked up with sad eyes. "You're so lucky to be young and free. Sometimes I'd do anything to just turn back the clock."

Sophie nodded. She wanted to say, "Yeah, me too," but didn't. Instead she went to help the man at the counter. To her relief, the shop continued to be busy. And that helped to pass the time. Occasionally she'd glance over to see the pregnant woman still sitting there with her feet propped up on the table. She was reading *Better Homes and Gardens* and probably dreaming of better days.

Finally it was a quarter to four and Marge came back. "Bless you for helping out like this," Marge told her as she slid her purse into the cabinet under the counter. She smiled and pointed to a slightly off-colored tooth. "The dentist gave me this temporary cap. The permanent one is supposed to look nicer."

"Better watch out for those Corn Nuts."

Marge grinned, then glanced over at the pregnant woman. "Is that the red minivan?"

Sophie nodded. "She's having a really hard day."

"I can imagine."

"She might need a little TLC." Sophie grabbed up her bag. "I have to get to a yearbook meeting."

"You run along, honey. And thanks!"

Sophie took one last look at the pregnant woman and dashed out of the tire store. Once outside, she gulped in a huge breath of fresh air. Whether it was the tire fumes or seeing that oversized belly, Sophie was feeling nauseated. And she so didn't want to have to explain why she had suddenly hurled in her dad's parking lot.

She got into her car, opened all the windows, and quickly drove away. She'd barely gone two blocks when she knew she could go no farther. She pulled to the curb, jumped out of the car, and hurled right onto the street. A school bus passed by slowly, and the kids inside were laughing and shrieking and pointing out their windows like she was the funniest thing since SpongeBob SquarePants.

Finally she was done. But as she was getting back into her car, she realized that she'd splattered vomit on her shoes. Just great. Now she could go to the yearbook meeting smelling like barf. Maybe Wes would be sorry he'd coerced her into another year of working on the yearbook.

7

For the next few weeks, Sophie lived in a constant state of fear, anxiety, and general hopelessness. Just to be sure, she'd purchased another home pregnancy kit, only to get the same positive results. Why they called the results *positive* was a mystery to her. Being seventeen and pregnant was anything but positive. It was, in fact, the most negative thing she'd ever experienced. Seriously, she would have rather been diagnosed with terminal cancer or run over by a freight train. Anything would be preferable to this.

Naturally she disguised these raw emotions in a cloak of humor, wit, and sarcasm. Then she topped it all off with a big umbrella of denial. Despite bouts of "morning" sickness, which occurred at various times of the day, and despite a "very late" period and sore breasts and a need to use the restroom more frequently, she continued to tell herself that this wasn't really happening. She wasn't really pregnant. And she certainly was *not* going to have a baby.

She focused her attention on other things. Like being selected as the yearbook editor and working on the school paper. She put all her energy into these activities—almost as if her journalism success might somehow erase the reality she was unable to face.

"So how about you?" Carrie Anne was looking directly at Sophie, kind of like she was directing that question to her.

"Huh?" Sophie blinked.

"You're such a space case," Jenny teased.

"It's because she's too smart," Kelsey said. "You know, one of those airhead genius types."

"Thanks a lot." Sophie looked back at Carrie Anne. "So what was it you were asking me?"

"If you're going to the homecoming dance."

"Well, let me see." Sophie held up her hand and counted on her fingers. "First Jeremy Brock asked me to go. Next was Caleb Stanton. And then there was—"

"Yeah, right." Jenny laughed.

"How the jocks love me," Sophie continued. "Let me count the ways."

"There are guys besides jocks," Carrie Anne pointed out.

"Duh." Sophie made a face. "Do you honestly think I'd go out with a jock anyway? I mean, I've turned down at least a dozen invitations—"

"So I'll take that as a no?" Carrie Anne said with a sly smile.

Sophie nodded. "That is definitely a no."

"Good."

Sophie frowned. "Thanks a lot. I thought you were my friend."

"It's good because I have something to ask you."

"You're asking me to go to the dance with you?" Sophie shook her head. "Sorry, Carrie Anne. I mean, I like you. But not like that."

Jenny and Kelsey laughed, but Carrie Anne did not look amused.

"Seriously, are you guys going to the dance?" Sophie looked at her friends.

"If you'd been paying attention, you'd know the answer to that one." Jenny gave a smug look.

"Meaning?"

"Meaning I'm going with John Hendricks," Jenny said. "And Kelsey is going with Timothy Banks."

Sophie frowned. They were a couple of guys from their youth group. Nice guys, but pretty shy. They rarely spoke to girls. "How'd you swing that?"

"Jenny asked them." Kelsey started to giggle.

Sophie stared at Jenny. "*You* asked them?"

"Yeah. And they agreed. It'll be a double date."

Sophie shrugged. "Well, good for you."

"Anyway . . ." Carrie Anne still seemed to have something on her mind. "Do you want to go to the dance, Sophie?"

"Like I said, Carrie Anne, I like you, but—"

"Not with me, you moron!"

"Who then?"

"Wes Andrews."

"Wes Andrews?" Sophie was shocked. "What do you mean?"

"I mean, he wants to ask you, but he's afraid you'll turn him down. Or that you won't want to be friends with him. Or something."

Sophie frowned. "So he talked to you?"

"Yeah, he asked me to sound you out. Of course, he didn't want me to tell you that he wanted to know." She laughed. "Like that was going to happen."

"For a smart kid, Wes is a little slow on the uptake," Jenny said.

"Or maybe he's just shy," Sophie said in his defense.

"So, what do you think?" Carrie Anne looked hopeful.

"Why do you care so much?" Sophie studied her friend. "I know—you like Wes and you want him to take you to the dance?"

"You are so lame."

Now Sophie felt indignant. "Are you saying you're too good for Wes?"

"No. I'm saying he wants to take you. And I want to know if you'll go or not."

"But why do you care?"

"I know why," Jenny said.

"Why?" the others all said at once.

"Because Carrie Anne likes Drew." Jenny nodded.

"Drew, as in Wes's best friend, Drew?" Sophie asked.

"Drew Valdez," Kelsey said. "Of course, it makes perfect sense."

"You like Drew?" Sophie asked Carrie Anne.

She kind of shrugged. "He's nice. He's an academic assistant for Mr. Cromwell. He's been helping me with my math."

Sophie chuckled. "And if you don't pass practical math, you can kiss your diploma bye-bye."

"Thanks for reminding me. But I'm doing just fine." Carrie Anne looked hopefully at Sophie. "So, will you?"

"Will I what?"

"Go to the homecoming dance with Wes?"

"I don't—"

"Have a heart, Sophie," Carrie Anne pleaded.

"Yeah, don't be such a wet blanket," Jenny said.

"It's not like we're asking you to marry the poor guy," Kelsey chimed in.

Jenny nodded. "Yeah, just go to the stupid dance."

"Come on," Carrie Anne begged. "You're my best friend. How often do I ask you to do anything for me?"

"Seriously?" Sophie was about ready to list all the things.

"It'll be fun," Kelsey said. "It's our senior year, and we should do some of these things. Come on, Sophie."

"Fine," Sophie snapped at them. "I'll go." She turned to Carrie Anne. "But only if it's a double date with you and Drew. Otherwise count me out."

Carrie Anne stuck out her hand. "Deal."

Sophie shook it halfheartedly. "Yeah, whatever."

The other three began talking about what they would wear, and Sophie stood. "Later," she said quickly. "I have to get something from my locker." She hurried on her way. She hoped she could make it to the restroom near the locker bay. It was usually the least busy. But before she could round the corner to get there, she knew it was too late. Fortunately there was a trash can handy. She grabbed hold of it and promptly lost her lunch.

"Nasty!" A girl nearby made a disgusted face.

"That's one way to lose a couple pounds," her friend said.

"Nice shot, babe." Naturally this came from a jock. Then he plugged his nose as he hurried past.

Sophie ignored them and continued on to the bathroom, where she rinsed out her mouth, splashed her face with water, and fished a box of breath mints out of her bag. She popped two in her mouth and headed for class.

As she walked by a bulletin board, she stopped. There, right next to a flyer about homecoming queen elections, was a totally different sort of flyer.

Unwanted pregnancy?

- Your body, your choice
- A woman's right to decide
- You have questions, we have answers
- Don't wait until it's too late

She stared at the bold slug lines. These people were not beating around the bush. She looked at the very bottom of the poster to see, in a much smaller font, the address and phone number of the free family planning clinic.

Sophie turned away and sighed. She knew exactly where that particular clinic was located. She'd gone there numerous times with Carrie Anne and her family. They would gather on the sidewalk in front to pray and to protest against the abortions performed. She had even carried a sign with a colored photograph of an unborn baby while picketing there. She'd tried to talk young women out of going inside that terrible place. She'd tried to make them understand that just because a baby was unborn didn't mean that it wasn't a living human being.

But she wasn't so sure anymore. Not about anything. Mostly she was confused and frightened. And she was beginning to understand why a woman would even consider such a horrendous act. Not that she was considering it herself. Not really.

❁

Sophie honestly did not remember driving there. She didn't even remember leaving school, getting into her car, driving across town, and finally pulling up into the parking lot in back. But as she got out of her car, she knew exactly where she was. And as she went through the back door and down a dimly lit corridor, she knew exactly what she was doing. At least, that was what she told herself.

Her hands shook as she filled out the form. But it was like a part of her had shut down. She wasn't sure whether it was her head or her heart, or perhaps it was both. She filled out the lines in a mechanical way, as if she was on some kind of automatic pilot. Or as if she was dead.

Maybe she was dead. If she was, then what she was about to do could not be considered murder. Because you couldn't kill something that wasn't even alive. Right?

Like a robot she went to the counter and slid the clipboard to the receptionist. The woman smiled, but it was a sad smile, a knowing smile—a smile that had probably given up a long time (and a lot of babies) ago.

"You might want to read these while you wait to see the counselor," the woman said as she slid a couple of pamphlets toward Sophie.

Sophie nodded. "Thanks." Then, still moving on autopilot, she made her way back to the seating area, which thankfully was empty. She sat down and attempted to focus her eyes on the material in her hand, but it seemed to jump out at her in blips and spurts. "Half of all pregnancies are unplanned . . . one in three women have had abortions . . . morning-after pill . . . aspiration . . . vacuum . . ."

Sophie set the pamphlets on the coffee table next to a bunch of others. Maybe everyone left the pamphlets behind. Who would want to take that with them? Who would want anyone to know?

"Sophie Ramsay?"

Sophie jumped, then looked around. Who knew she was here?

"Sophie?"

Sophie realized it was the receptionist. "Yes?"

"The counselor will see you now." She nodded toward a hallway. "The second door down."

Sophie slowly stood, glancing left and right and wondering if she should just make a run for it. Get out of there before she was sorry. But she'd left her name and phone number on that form. What if they called her at home? What if they told her parents? Why hadn't she thought of this sooner? She'd always heard that these places kept people's names anonymous. But what if she was wrong? What if that was just a trick?

"Excuse me." She paused by the receptionist's desk.

"Yes?"

"I forgot to ask you something."

"Well, the counselor is the best one to answer your—"

"No, I mean about the form I filled out."

"Oh, was there a mistake?"

"No. I mean, is it confidential?"

The woman frowned. "Well, the counselor and the doctor will have to—"

"No, I mean confidential outside of this office. Like will my parents be informed that I came—"

"Oh, don't worry about that, dear."

"Really? You don't notify them at all?"

"Not unless you ask us to."

"Honestly?"

"Honestly. Your secret is safe with us."

Sophie sighed. "Okay."

"Don't worry."

"Right." Sophie nodded.

"The counselor is waiting, dear."

She nodded again. As she walked down the hallway, she tried to grasp what she'd just heard. How was it possible that she, a minor, could undergo a surgical procedure that ended a human life while her parents remained totally clueless, yet just last spring when Sophie had gone to the school nurse due to menstrual cramps, the nurse had refused to administer Advil without calling Sophie's mom first? Not that she'd wanted her parents to know exactly. But it just didn't make sense that an abortion was perfectly permissible without parental consent when a simple over-the-counter pain reliever was not. It was actually kind of creepy when she thought about it.

"Sophie Ramsay?" A short, dark-haired woman extended her hand. "I'm Mary."

"Hi." Sophie attempted a weak smile.

"Come into my office and let's chat."

Chat? Sophie wasn't really sure she wanted to chat. Mostly she just wanted to end this thing. But perhaps it was required to chat first.

Mary sat down at a cluttered desk and looked at the form still on the clipboard. "You're seventeen?"

"Yes. Is that a problem?"

Mary smiled faintly. "I guess it depends on your perspective."

"You mean seventeen and pregnant?"

She nodded. "And you're certain that you're pregnant?"

Sophie explained the test. How she did it once with only six seconds of flow, then did it again, and then did it a third time with another test. "But it was the same result every time—they were all positive. Do you think I did it wrong?"

Mary just made another note.

"I thought the first test was an old one. The box looked kind of old, and I got it from this weird little drugstore, and . . . well, I wondered, do those tests have some kind of a shelf life?"

"Sometimes a test can be faulty."

"The second test, well, I accidentally dropped one wand in the toilet. And then the other one was, well, positive."

"It wouldn't hurt to be retested."

"Like maybe I'm not really—"

"When was your last period?" Mary skimmed the form, then pointed to the line that Sophie had filled in. "The first week of August?"

"I think so. I wasn't really paying attention, you know. But I'd been at this camp—a youth camp I worked at during August— for about a few days, I think."

"Uh-huh." She read down the form. "And you were sexually active afterward?"

"Well, I wouldn't call it that. I mean, yes, I had sex. But it was the first time. I mean, I'd been a virgin until then."

"You got pregnant the first time you had sex?" Mary looked dubious.

"I'd heard you couldn't get pregnant the first time."

Mary shook her head. "That's not true."

"Oh."

"So you got pregnant the first time you had sex?"

"I don't know. I mean, I didn't think it was possible. And then I had sex again."

"So you were sexually active."

"No. I only did it twice."

"So . . . ," Mary looked slightly impatient, ". . . you're saying you had sex twice and you got pregnant?"

"That's what happened."

"Okay." Mary picked up a pencil and fluttered it between her fingers. "So, can I assume that you didn't use protection?"

"Not the first time."

"The second time?"

"He had a condom . . . but it broke."

"And he didn't have a spare?"

Sophie just shook her head.

Mary wrote something down on a little pad. She ripped it off and handed it to Sophie.

"What's this?"

"A prescription for birth control."

"I don't need this." Had Mary even been listening to her?

"Maybe you don't need it right now, but after—"

"No. I won't ever need it. I don't plan on having sex again."

"Ever?"

"Not until I get married. And I don't plan on getting married until I'm . . . at least thirty."

"You don't say."

"Seriously." Sophie shoved the paper back at her. "I don't need this."

"You didn't need it before . . . before August?"

"No. I just should've stuck to my pledge."

"Let me guess—you made an abstinence pledge?"

"A purity pledge."

"Would you be surprised to hear that a lot of girls make and break that same pledge? And that a lot of girls end up sitting right where you are telling me the exact same story?"

"The exact same story?"

"Well, not exactly. But they don't plan on having sex. They're committed to wait until marriage. But then something happens. A boyfriend pressures them. They have an irrepressible urge. Even date rape."

Sophie sat up straighter. She could feel tears coming on again.

"Then they're pregnant. And scared and desperate."

"Like me."

"Yes." She held out the prescription again. "You're sure you don't want this?"

"I'm positive."

"It's your choice."

"My body. My choice." Sophie heard the sarcasm in her voice.

"So you're positive you want to terminate this pregnancy?"

Sophie nodded, trying to appear confident. And trying to shut down that little voice that was inside of her, screaming, *Stop! Stop! Stop this nonsense and get out of this place NOW!*

"Because adoption is an option."

"Not for me." Sophie resisted the urge to cover her ears with her hands—not that it would make any difference, since the words she wanted to block were on the inside, not the outside.

"I understand." Mary made a note on Sophie's form, then looked up. "Do you have any questions about the procedure?"

"I read the brochures." Okay, that was a lie. But then, wasn't everything about her life a big fat lie now?

Shut up! Shut up! Shut up! Had she actually said those words aloud?

But Mary just nodded. "Good," she said. "I'm glad you took the time."

"So is that it then?"

Mary sighed. "I guess that's it. Unless you have any questions." She waited while Sophie tried to think of something to ask. "But if you don't . . ."

"I don't." Sophie wanted to tell Mary to hurry it up, that if they waited one minute longer, it could be too late and that inner voice would have its way. Or else Sophie might lose her mind. Unless she'd already lost it.

"Okay then. I'll pass this information on to the doctor. We'll schedule you for a physical and—"

"*Schedule* me?"

"Yes. That's how it works."

"You mean I can't have it today?" Sophie's hands fisted so tightly that her nails dug into her palms.

"Well, you can check with the receptionist. They might be able to fit in a physical."

"Just a physical? What about—what about the—the procedure?"

"The abortion?"

"Yes. I mean, I thought that I was going to have it *today*."

"Today?"

"Yes!" Sophie felt like she was falling, tumbling down into a pitch-black hole of hopelessness. "That's why I came!"

"I understand your sense of urgency. Trust me, you're not alone."

"But I *am* alone." Sophie was crying now.

"I know it's an emotional time. But you need to be examined by the doctor, and he may want to do another pregnancy test just to be sure—"

Sophie's legs were shaking as she stood up. "I need to go."

"Don't forget to make an appointment with the—"

"No." Sophie's voice was too loud. "Of course I won't forget." Then she walked out of Mary's office and right past the receptionist's desk. Without saying a word, she turned down the dark corridor and headed straight for the back door. She felt numb as she exited the building and got into her car.

As if on autopilot, she drove home, where she intended to simply lie down on her bed and just die. After all, she was partially dead already, right?

8

"Why'd you blow off yearbook committee yesterday?" Wes asked Sophie during journalism class.

"I had a dentist appointment." Another lie. Not that she was counting anymore. But Sophie knew she wasn't a good liar. She kept her eyes on the computer screen, pretending to be absorbed in her work as she made some final tweaks to the front page of next week's paper.

"You could've told someone."

"I forgot."

"Are you okay, Sophie?"

She looked blankly at him. What was he insinuating here? Did he suspect something? Was he able to see right past her cloak of deception? Just the same, she would not give him an inch. She scowled. "Do I not look okay?"

He made a crooked smile. "You look great. But that headline is a little strange." He pointed to the screen and chuckled.

She stared at the headline that she'd just pasted and read it aloud. "'Who Will Wear the Crow?'" She frowned. "Huh?"

"I think you dropped an *n*."

"Oh yeah. 'Who Will Wear the Crown?'" She shook her head. "Duh."

"But I do think it'd be amusing to see Katie Dannon wearing a crow on her head."

"What makes you think Katie Dannon is going to win?"

"Just a hunch."

Sophie inserted the *n* and hit save.

"Uh, speaking of homecoming . . ." Wes cleared his throat. "And crows."

"Yeah . . . homecoming and crows."

Sophie knew where he was going with this. She had to come up with a nice way to turn him down. Carrie Anne or not, Sophie did not want to go to that dance.

"I know you're probably going to say forget it," he began. "And I wouldn't really blame you. I just hope you won't hold it against me for asking. I mean, you're the coolest girl I know, and . . ." His voice trailed off.

Now she felt guilty. "I'm the coolest girl you know?" she said.

He nodded. "Yeah. And I was just hoping that maybe you'd want to go to the dance with me. I mean, just as friends."

"Just as friends?" She looked curiously at him.

"Not that I don't want to be more than friends. I mean . . . well, I like you, Sophie. You're fun and you're funny and you're real, you know?"

She didn't know what to say. Why did he have to be so sweet about it? He was making this difficult.

"So, if you're going to turn me down, could you, like, just get it over with?" He smiled nervously.

"Okay, fine," she said. "I'll go with you."

"Really?"

Had she just agreed to go with him? She'd heard the words come out of her mouth, but it wasn't what she'd meant to say. What was wrong with her anyway? Did being pregnant mess with your head as much as it messed with your body?

"You're not just jerking me around?" His eyes looked larger than usual behind his dark-rimmed glasses. Sophie studied the color—kind of a blue-green-gray. "You'll really go to the dance with me?"

"I guess." She sighed. "But on one condition."

He frowned. "One condition?"

"Carrie Anne wants to go to the dance with Drew, and unless that happens I won't—"

"Not a problem." He grinned.

"Seriously?"

"Yeah. Drew thinks Carrie Anne is hot."

"He does?"

Wes nodded. "Looks like it's kind of a slam dunk then?"

"Maybe so." She forced a smile. "Want me to wear a crow on my head?"

He laughed. "No, you should leave that to Katie Dannon."

"Sophie?"

She looked over to see Mr. Young motioning to her. "Yeah?"

He nodded toward his office. "I need to speak to you."

"You're in trouble now." Wes winked at her.

She slowly stood and walked toward the office. She knew it was unlikely that she was really in trouble, not seriously. But for some reason her heart was pounding like she was. She knew it was impossible that Mr. Young had any idea about what was going on with her, yet she felt like he did. Each step felt heavy with guilt, like her feet were thudding so loudly on the floor that everyone in the classroom was listening, watching, like they knew.

What if the family planning clinic had called the school to reach her? It was unreasonable and unlikely, but *what if?* What if Mary had blabbed to someone in the counseling center, saying that Sophie Ramsay was about six weeks pregnant and that she needed to schedule an appointment for an abortion ASAP? What if the whole world knew it by now?

"Come on in," Mr. Young said.

Sophie went into the office. Her knees felt shaky, and her stomach seemed to be following suit. Hopefully she wasn't about to hurl. She glanced at the wastebasket by his desk.

He closed the door. "I want to keep this private."

She felt her throat constricting.

"As you know, I haven't selected the chief editor for the paper yet."

She just nodded and stared down at the wastebasket. *Don't hurl, don't hurl, don't hurl,* she told herself.

"To be perfectly honest, I had planned to ask you to fill this position."

She looked up with wide eyes. "Had planned?" Did he know something?

He cocked his head slightly to one side. "Are you feeling okay?"

She took in a quick breath and forced a shaky smile. "Yeah, sure."

He nodded but looked skeptical. "As I was saying, I had planned to ask you to be chief editor, Sophie. You're the most qualified for the job, and before school started, I figured it was a no-brainer."

She didn't know what to say. What was his point? Even if he did know she was pregnant, which really seemed unlikely, would he use that to discriminate against her? And if so, would she fight it? Could she?

"But then school began, and, well, it just doesn't seem like you have the same kind of enthusiasm you've exhibited in the past." He studied her. "Something about you seems to have changed. Or maybe you've just decided that journalism isn't where it's at anymore."

"I love journalism."

"That's a relief."

She pressed her lips together.

"Is everything okay with you, Sophie?"

She shrugged. "Yeah, sure."

"Something going on in your personal life?"

Without making eye contact, she just shook her head.

He sort of chuckled. "It's not that I want to hear about your love life or anything like that. But I do know that it's not easy being a teenager. Never has been. And hearts get broken right and left." He just stood there with his hands in his pockets, as if he was unsure how to proceed.

"If I've seemed less enthusiastic," she began carefully, "it's not because I've lost interest. I mean, really, I do love journalism. But . . . you're right, I am going through something—kind of a broken heart. I just really don't want to talk about it, okay?" She looked him in the eyes, and he actually seemed relieved.

"That's what I suspected." He smiled. "If it's any consolation, these things always get better with time."

"Thanks." But all she could think was that this particular thing would only get bigger with time—and much, much worse.

"And sometimes the best medicine is to lose yourself in something you love, like journalism. It's a good distraction." He put a hand on her shoulder. "So, what do you think? Do you want to be this year's chief editor?"

Whether it was the kindness in his voice or the touch of his hand, something in her just shattered, and she knew she was about to cry. Without answering him, she turned and dashed from his office, tore out of the journalism room, and headed straight for the bathroom and into a stall. Not to barf but to bawl.

As Sophie was blowing her nose, she heard a tapping sound. "Huh?"

"It's Justina," a quiet voice said. "Mr. Young sent me to check on you."

Justina Coughlin was another journalism geek. Shy and unsure of herself, she sometimes loomed behind Sophie, quietly observing as Sophie worked on something. She reminded Sophie of a shadow.

"I'm fine," Sophie said.

"Are you sick or something?"

Sophie opened the door and stared at Justina. She was about the same height as Sophie, but stick-thin and not in the model-cool way. With stringy, dishwater-blonde hair and a complexion that resembled a childhood disease, Justina wasn't exactly a head turner. "I'm fine," Sophie said again.

"Were you crying?"

Sophie shrugged as she went for the sink, ran cold water, and splashed it onto her face.

"Did Mr. Young say something mean to you?"

Sophie tore off a paper towel, dried her face, and turned back to Justina. "No, he didn't say anything *mean*. Not that it's any of your business, but he asked me to be chief editor."

"Oh." Justina looked confused and hurt, and Sophie felt guilty.

"I'm sorry," Sophie said quickly. "It's not your fault."

"So . . . you're upset because Mr. Young asked you to be chief editor?"

"Not exactly." Sophie sighed. "Maybe I'm just hormonal."

"PMS?" Justina pressed. "I know what you mean. I get it really bad too. My mom's the same way."

"Yeah." Sophie nodded as if that was the problem. If only that *was* the problem.

"Do you want to go back to class now?"

"Not really."

"Yeah, I don't blame you. It's probably pretty embarrassing." Justina brightened. "Want me to get your stuff for you?"

Sophie considered this. It's not like she could just skip out on class and expect no consequences. What if someone called her parents? The last thing she needed was for them to be questioning her.

"I can tell Mr. Young that you're not feeling good."

Sophie nodded. "Yeah, would you do that?"

"If you go to the counselor and tell her you have a bad case of PMS, she'll write you an excuse."

"Seriously?"

"Yeah. I had to do that once. Actually, this girl had teased me, and, well, I was already having a crappy day and I kind of fell apart. But Mrs. Phelps was really nice about it. She's really understanding."

Sophie waited in the restroom while Justina returned to get Sophie's things. She wondered what exactly Justina would say to Mr. Young. Hopefully she wouldn't mention hormones or PMS. And what if Wes asked what was up? What would Justina tell him?

As embarrassing as it would be, maybe the smartest thing would be for Sophie to simply return and face the music. She could make a joke about it. Act like she'd been so touched by being asked to be chief editor that she'd gotten emotional. Of course, then she'd need to respond to the offer. Was she willing to be chief editor? Would it be better to just pass? Or would that draw even more unwanted attention?

"Here you go." Justina handed Sophie her bag and the hoodie that she'd left behind.

"Thanks." Sophie pulled on her sweatshirt and looped the strap of her bag over her shoulder.

"Mr. Young asked me to escort you."

"Escort me?" Sophie frowned.

"Yeah. I made it sound like you were sick. I didn't think you'd want me to mention PMS, you know?"

Sophie nodded. "Oh yeah, thanks."

"So I'll just walk you there, okay?"

So Justina Coughlin escorted Sophie to the counseling center. She felt like she was about six years old when Justina knocked on Mrs. Phelps's door and introduced Sophie. "She's having really bad PMS," Justina said in an undertone. "I told her you could help."

Mrs. Phelps smiled and waved Sophie in.

"Thanks," Sophie said crisply to Justina, as if she could handle it from here. Once Justina was gone, Sophie closed the door and sat down in the chair across from Mrs. Phelps, letting out a big sigh.

"Having a hard day?" Mrs. Phelps asked.

"Make that a hard life."

Mrs. Phelps removed her reading glasses and peered curiously at Sophie. "Want to talk about it?"

Now Sophie regretted her previous statement.

"I know that hormones can play havoc with our emotions sometimes." Mrs. Phelps pushed a strand of auburn hair behind an ear and sighed. "Trust me, I *know*."

Sophie nodded. "Yeah, I kind of lost it in journalism."

Her brows lifted slightly. "Did you let someone have it?"

"Not exactly. I kind of fell apart and started to cry."

"Oh, that can be even worse than losing your temper."

"Pretty humiliating."

"What made you fall apart?" Mrs. Phelps leaned back in her chair. "I mean, besides PMS."

"I'm not really sure. Mr. Young was being nice. He'd just asked me to be chief editor of the paper."

"Congratulations."

Sophie bit her lip.

"Or not . . ."

"I'm just not sure I should do it."

"Why not?"

Sophie shrugged but didn't answer.

"You shouldn't allow your current emotional state to frighten you out of doing something you really want to do." She smiled.

"I make it a firm rule not to make any major life decisions when I'm in the midst of PMS. It's kind of like getting your hair cut when you're having a bad hair day—it can turn out to be a big mistake. You just need to be patient and wait until the emotions pass."

"What if they *don't* pass?"

"Oh, they always pass . . . eventually."

Sophie didn't say anything, just looked down at her hands and frowned.

"Sophie?"

"Huh?" Sophie looked up to see that Mrs. Phelps looked slightly concerned. With her chin in her hand, she studied Sophie carefully, almost like she was taking some kind of inventory. Or perhaps she could see right through her.

"Is this something else, something besides PMS?"

Sophie shook her head. "No . . . not at all."

"Are you sure?"

Sophie looked back down again.

"You can talk to me."

"I know."

"Anything you say to me will be confidential."

Sophie looked back up.

"You can trust me."

You can trust me. Sophie's face grew hot as she remembered the last time she'd heard those four words . . . from Dylan. *You can trust me.* Yeah, right.

"It will help to talk," Mrs. Phelps continued. "I'm a good listener."

"Thanks." Sophie reached for her bag. "I'll keep that in mind." She stood and took a deep breath. "I feel better now."

Mrs. Phelps nodded with a sad expression. Or maybe it was disappointment.

"Do I need to get an excuse or something? I mean, for missing class just now."

She wrote something down on a pad. "Yes, I'll take care of it."

"Thanks."

"And if you change your mind and need to—"

"I know—you're a good listener." The problem, she almost said, was that she was not ready to talk about it—to God or anyone.

9

"Are you sick?" Carrie Anne asked in an impatient tone.

"Hello to you too." Sophie was tempted to hang up. Seriously, what kind of a greeting was that?

"Sorry, but I'm serious. Are you?"

"What?"

"Sick."

"No, but thanks for caring."

"I do care. It's just that Wes said you got sick in journalism."

"You talked to Wes?" Sophie peeled her eyes off of her computer screen to see that it was after ten and she still wasn't finished.

"Well, yeah. He told me that you'd agreed to go to the homecoming dance with him, then you got sick and ran off. Like was that a coincidence?"

"Meaning?"

"Meaning Wes is worried that he made you sick."

Despite herself, Sophie laughed. "Seriously?"

"I told him that was ridiculous. So what happened then? Why did he think you were sick?"

Sophie told Carrie Anne about talking to Mr. Young in his office, making it seem like the way he'd questioned her interest in being the chief editor had been upsetting. It actually seemed not only fairly clever but rather believable as well. "I just overreacted," she said finally. "I think it was PMS."

"I don't blame you for overreacting, Sophie. You're the obvious choice for chief editor. I can't believe he'd even question you on that."

"I know."

"I hope you stood up for yourself."

"That's a little hard to do when you're bawling."

"You were bawling?" Carrie Anne sounded alarmed.

"Not in front of him. I did have the good sense to get to the restroom."

"Well, I'm sure you can straighten it all out with him tomorrow."

"Maybe."

"Just tell him that he hurt your feelings and that you're the right woman for the job. I mean, journalism is, like, in your blood. He should know better."

Suddenly Sophie wished she hadn't twisted the truth so much. Mostly she just wanted to change the subject before it got worse. "So, what's up with Drew now? I told Wes that the only way I'd go to the dance with him was if we doubled with you and Drew."

"That must've been flattering. Way to boost a guy's ego."

"He understood." Sophie sighed. "But back to Drew. Did he ask you to the dance or what?"

"As a matter of fact, he did. Because, unlike a certain best friend who shall remain unnamed, *I* went to youth group tonight."

"I told you I had to finish this project."

"But you've missed youth group for two weeks in a row, Sophie."

"So take away my gold star, all right?"

"Well, you really should schedule your time better. I mean, you have most of the afternoon off, it seems like you should be able to get your homework done—"

"I'm also on yearbook, remember?" The truth was, Sophie had skipped out on that today too. Part of her "sick" routine.

"Whatever. Just the same, you need fellowship."

"I'm talking to you, right? Isn't that fellowship?"

"I suppose."

"Anyway, I'm guessing Drew was at youth group."

"He was. And he met me at the door and asked me straight out, which turned out to be a good thing since I think he was too embarrassed to talk to me much afterward."

"So the four of us are going to the dance now? It's all settled?"

"You make it sound like some cut-and-dried business deal. It's a dance, Sophie. It's supposed to be fun."

"Yeah, right. It's a dance that I've been coerced by my best friend to go to. What fun."

"You seriously need to lighten up, Sophie."

"I seriously need to finish this opinion piece for journalism tomorrow. It's bad enough that I made a total fool of myself and ran out of there like a baby. I really need to be able to hold my head up tomorrow."

"Well, you go, girl."

"Thanks."

"And thanks for telling Wes you'd go to the dance."

"Right. Now you owe me."

"I owe, I owe," Carrie Anne sang like one of the dwarfs in *Snow White*, "so off to bed I go."

"Very cute, Dopey."

"Night night, Grumpy."

Sophie returned to her opinion piece, rereading it from the beginning and then cutting about a third of it. Tighten, tighten, tighten. Her topic was school security. Or rather the lack of it. Sure, their school put on the appearance of being safe and secure, with a part-time guard wandering around in uniform, but the kids knew it was all show and no go. If someone really wanted to sneak homemade bombs or automatic weapons into the school, it wouldn't be all that hard.

Finally satisfied, or perhaps just tired, Sophie hit save and then print. Once the doc was printed, she shut off her computer and crawled into bed.

She missed her old routine of reading the Bible and praying before going to sleep. But after two weeks of skipping, she was slowly getting used to it. Didn't they say it took only two weeks to make or break a habit? Still, it got harder and harder to shut down her mind and go to sleep. During the day, she could distract herself from reality, but her worst fears always seemed to confront her at night.

It was during the night that she reconsidered the whole abortion thing. Sure, she had run out of that horrible clinic with the certainty that abortion had always been—and still was—wrong, wrong, wrong. Taking a human life to cover up your own stupid mistake was wrong, wrong, wrong. She was able to convince herself—during the daylight hours—that she would never, never, never kill an unborn child.

But that all got blurry and gray when she turned the lights out. Like demons coming out in the darkness, her doubts and fears would torment her until she thought the only answer was to simply end this thing. Sometimes she imagined ending it even more completely than simply having an abortion—she imagined ending her own life as well. That way no one would ever know. Her shame would be buried with her. Well, unless someone did an autopsy. What then?

And on she would go—round and round until she finally succumbed to sleep. But that escape was only temporary because, almost like clockwork, her bladder would demand to be emptied at four a.m. And after that, wide-awake, she would be tortured anew.

Finally morning would come, and as if frightened by the light, these demons and doubts would all scurry away. Well, for the most part. She was still plagued with one major fear: what if someone found out? What would she do?

Every morning after her shower, Sophie would peel back her robe and examine herself in the full-length mirror on her closet door. She knew her body was changing, be it ever so slightly. Her curves seemed curvier and fuller. Her stomach was rounded a bit more. She knew no one else could see these changes, and she tended to carry extra weight anyway, so she'd probably be able to conceal it for longer than most. But she also knew it wouldn't be long before the changes were obvious. And what then?

Sophie had heard of teenage girls who'd gone full-term in their pregnancies without anyone knowing. She'd read stories of how girls had delivered their babies by themselves . . . and how some even killed their infants and hid them in dumpsters. But it seemed that they were eventually found out. How else did it make the news?

Sophie knew that, although she wanted to hide her secret forever, she wasn't about to murder an innocent baby and drop it in a dumpster. At least she knew that in the light of day. Sometimes, at night, her imagination ran away with her.

"Sophie?" her mother said with impatience.

"Huh?" Sophie looked up from her bowl of soggy Cheerios and frowned.

"I just asked you if you knew what time it is."

"What time it is?"

Her mother shook her head and pointed to the clock. "You're going to be late for school."

"Oh!" Sophie stood up, reaching for the bowl.

"Just leave it," her mom said.

"Thanks." Sophie pulled on her denim jacket and grabbed her bag.

"Don't drive too fast either."

"Yeah, yeah."

"And don't be such a space cadet!" she called out as Sophie ran for the door.

As Sophie drove to school, she thought about Dylan. She didn't want to think about him, but she couldn't help herself. After all, wasn't he equally to blame for her condition? Shouldn't he have to share some of the trouble she was enduring? Shouldn't he feel a little freaked-out too? Not for the first time, she considered calling him up and telling him the news. How would she say it?

"Hey, Dylan, just wanted to congratulate you."

"For what?" he'd ask.

"You're going to be a daddy."

Yeah, right. In her dreams. And in her dreams, Dylan would come to his senses and offer to do—what? Marry her? No, she definitely didn't want to marry a guy who had not only deceived her and used her but totally messed up her life. A guy who probably couldn't care less. She knew that, according to the law, he bore some responsibility, but did she really want some court to force him into paying? And really, what would he pay for—her medical expenses? Not that she had any. Her maternity clothes? Like she was even going there. An abortion, perhaps? No thanks!

The truth was, there was one major reason she was not telling Dylan about her "delicate condition." Plain and simple, she did not want to tell him because that would be the beginning—the beginning of the end. She knew that if she told Dylan, his parents would probably have to be informed as well. And that meant her parents would find out. Then everyone would find out. Then her life would be, well, basically over. She just couldn't handle that. Not yet.

No, she decided, the best thing was to pretend this wasn't happening, and to do so for as long as humanly possible. She would attempt to enjoy (a gross overstatement) the last shreds of her totally ruined life. If she got lucky, maybe she would get in a car wreck or fall down some stairs and suffer a miscarriage, and no one would be the wiser. Well, no one except her. And God. Of course, God knew everything. Not that he seemed to care much.

She parked in the school lot and jogged toward the building. There by the front door, watching her like he knew what she'd written last night, stood a grim-faced security guard.

"Looks like someone slept in this morning." His voice was pseudo cheerful, but his expression was coated with disapproval.

She just rolled her eyes and hurried past. As she whizzed by the counseling center, she nearly collided with Mrs. Phelps, who was coming out the door.

"Sophie!"

"Sorry." She stopped. "I'm late."

"I can see that." Mrs. Phelps put a hand on Sophie's arm. "Everything okay?"

"Just peachy."

The counselor frowned.

"I really am late."

"Hurry along then."

As Sophie slipped into the classroom, taking a seat in the back, she suddenly remembered a sweater that Grandma Ramsay had knit for her when Sophie was in first grade. The pullover had been pale pink and softer than a kitten, and Sophie had loved it. Then one day she noticed a string of yarn hanging from the sleeve. Wanting to get rid of the messy thing, she tugged at it. But the yarn only grew longer. She pulled more, and as the yarn grew longer, the sleeve grew shorter. Fascinated by the growing pile of yarn in her lap, Sophie continued to pull and pull until her sweater eventually became sleeveless on one side. She knew the sweater was ruined, and with no idea of how to fix it, she tossed the tangled ball of soft pink yarn in the trash. Naturally she was teased without mercy that day—the girl in the one-armed sweater. Then at home, embarrassed that she'd destroyed her beloved sweater, she had hidden what was left of it in the back of her closet and never worn it again.

Today, that's how her life felt—she was unraveling, and quickly. And her ruination was her own fault. But it wasn't going to be as easily hidden as the ruined sweater. Not for long, anyway.

"You're being awfully quiet," Carrie Anne said to Sophie at the lunch table. "Still feeling sick?"

"You're sick?" Kelsey asked.

"Is it catching?" Jenny backed away from where she was sitting next to Sophie.

"I'm *not* sick," Sophie said.

"Just PMS," Carrie Anne said not so quietly.

"Thanks, Carrie," Sophie snapped. "Why not tell the whole world."

"Sorry."

"You weren't at youth group last night," Hannah pointed out.

"Thanks for letting me in on that." Sophie made a face.

"Why are you cutting youth group?" Jenny asked.

"Homework." Carrie Anne looked skeptical. "Or so she claims."

"Well, you missed the big talk." Hannah grinned.

"The big talk?" Sophie frowned.

"You know, the old back-to-school sex talk we get every year," Kelsey said.

Sophie chuckled. "Guess I didn't miss much then."

"I'll say," Jenny agreed. "And this year they took it to a whole new level."

"Huh?"

"Yeah," Carrie Anne said. "First Phil talked to us together like usual. Then he and Jeanette broke us into two groups."

"Girls and guys were separated," Hannah said.

Sophie shrugged. "That actually sounds smart."

"Except that Jeanette decided to get really explicit," Kelsey said.

"Explicit?" Sophie echoed.

"*Embarrassingly* explicit." Jenny giggled.

Carrie Anne lowered her voice. "Yeah, she really laid it on the line."

"How so?" Sophie leaned forward with interest.

"She defined sexual purity," Kelsey said. "Specifically."

"Specifically?"

"Uh-huh." Kelsey nodded.

"Meaning?"

"Like we're going to talk about that here." Carrie Anne glanced nervously around the noisy cafeteria.

"Come on," Sophie urged her friends. "Just tell me what she said."

"Like you even need to hear it," Jenny teased. "You're like the queen of abstinence anyway."

"Yeah," Kelsey agreed. "You don't even date."

"I had to practically threaten her to go to the homecoming dance," Carrie Anne added.

"So you are going?" Hannah asked.

And then they were all talking about the dance and what they were going to wear and how Carrie Anne's mom had already said the girls could make a special dinner at her house to save the boys some bucks. Then they were menu planning, and Sophie tried to act interested and like she was still one of them. She even promised to make cheesecake for dessert.

"We'll go dress shopping on Saturday," Kelsey said. "That way our dresses will all look good together."

Then they started to argue over skirt lengths and whether pastel or bright colors were cooler and what clashed with what. Sophie was relieved when the first bell rang and she was able to escape the planning frenzy.

"You'd think we were planning our weddings," Sophie said as she and Carrie Anne took their lunch trays to the drop-off area. "Why all this obsessive craziness?"

"Because it's fun. Plus it'll be good practice for the prom."

"So you're already planning to go to the prom now?" Sophie frowned as she dumped the remainder of her lunch in the garbage can.

"Why not?"

As Sophie dropped off her tray, she could think of dozens of reasons why not. At least where she was concerned. Prom was usually in late April or early May. By then Sophie would be full-term pregnant and probably bigger than a barn. By then all her friends and the universe at large would know her "little" secret. And by then Sophie would be a great big portion of supersized humiliation.

10

"Feeling better today?" Mr. Young asked.

Sophie gave him a big smile as she entered the classroom. She was ready for this now. No more dramatics—except for what she hoped would be an award-winning performance of normal. "Yeah, I'm feeling fine now. Thanks." She handed him her opinion piece. "Sorry about yesterday. I think I ate something bad at lunch or something."

"Well, I had one of their cheeseburgers today, and I can understand how that could happen." He chuckled, then glanced down at her paper and headed to his office.

She was relieved that he hadn't pressed her about the chief editor position again. Maybe he'd decided to forget about it after witnessing yesterday's meltdown. Really, wouldn't that be for the best? She suspected that Wes would be his second choice. And all things considered, Wes would probably be a lot more reliable. The obvious man for the job. Of course, that fact stung.

For the past three years, ever since she'd been involved in the school paper, the chief editors had all been guys. To be fair, there really hadn't been any girls who wanted to step up to the task. Except for her. Last year she'd made it clear that she was ready—and she'd even teased Mr. Young about discrimination based on gender. She'd actually written an op-ed piece on it. He'd run it in the paper alongside one of his own in which he'd assured her and everyone else that he did not discriminate against women. It had actually been quite convincing. As the year progressed, she had been hopeful that she'd be the first girl (for quite some time) to break the string of male domination on the paper. It seemed that she'd actually gotten her chance. Except she had ruined everything.

"Hey, Sophie," Wes said. "Feeling okay today?"

"Yeah, thanks."

"Justina said you got sick. Was it me?"

Sophie laughed. "Don't take yourself too seriously."

"You know what I mean . . . about the dance."

"No, it was not you, Wes. I think I ate something bad for lunch. That's all, okay?"

He brightened. "Okay."

Mr. Young cleared his throat and stepped up to the head of the classroom. "I've selected some of the opinion pieces to be read aloud today, followed by critiquing."

Back in the old days, Sophie had always been eager to take her turn and read something she'd written. Not now. She was glad when a couple of others were called to read first, and although she contributed to their critiques, she didn't want to be the one on the hot seat this time.

But after about five more pieces and critiques, she started to get worried. What if Mr. Young hadn't liked her piece? What if she was losing it as a writer? What if she was suddenly yesterday's news—a has-been, a pregnant loser chick no one would ever take seriously again? What if—

"Sophie Ramsay?" Mr. Young held up her piece. "You'll be our final reader."

Shaken but relieved not to have been totally excluded, Sophie took her paper and began to read. As she read, she could tell by the reaction of her listeners—laughter in appropriate spots and silence in others—that she was still hitting the mark. When she finished, they clapped. Actually clapped.

Sophie could feel herself beaming as she took her seat. When the critique began, she mostly got praise. Finally Mr. Young stepped in. "Sophie has nailed it," he told them. "And I'm going to tell you why. She picked one subject and stuck to it. She explained the problem with humor and insight. She kept it simple and succinct. She obviously did some research to support her opinion. And she wrote about a topic that concerns everyone." He smiled at her. "As a teacher, I'd give this piece an A plus. And as a publisher, I'd run it in the editor's column because I'm asking Sophie Ramsay to accept the position of chief editor. I've already asked Wes Andrews to assume the role of managing editor, which he has accepted."

He pointed to Sophie. "So, how about it? Don't you think it's about time this paper was run by a woman?"

She nodded. "I do."

He grinned. "Sophie Ramsay, I now pronounce you chief editor of the *Panther Paw*."

Wes started to clap, and when the rest joined in, it took every ounce of Sophie's self-control and composure to keep from crying. "Thanks," she told them in a husky voice. "As chief editor, I think we better get to work."

"That's right," Wes said. "We've got a paper to get out."

❀

The last thing Sophie wanted to spend her whole Saturday doing was trying on formals with her girlfriends. Shopping with friends who were thinner had never been good for her self-image in the first place, but watching them modeling all these strapless, backless, low-cut, figure-hugging dresses was making her want to lose her lunch.

"Come out," Carrie Anne urged her.

Sophie looked at her image in the mirror and frowned. "It's not working for me," she called back.

"Just let us see," Kelsey said. "I think that shade of coral is going to be great with your complexion."

"Fine." Sophie emerged from the room, held her hands out to her sides, and made a sour face. "I look like an overgrown pomegranate."

Her friends laughed.

"And speaking of fruit . . . ," she put her hands beneath her breasts and gave them a little push-up, ". . . these melons are about ready to bust out of here."

Her friends laughed harder, and she joked more. Of course, her jokes were all at her own expense. Not that anyone noticed. Besides her.

"It's useless," she said finally.

"No, it's not," Carrie Anne declared. "We just need to look harder."

"No." Sophie shook her head. "Not until you listen to me."

"What?"

"I don't want anything that's low-cut or strapless or backless or tight."

"Why don't you just wear your bathrobe?"

"Good idea."

"Seriously, Sophie," Carrie Anne said. "You sound like you want to go as a nun."

Sophie pointed at Carrie Anne. "And you look like you want to go as a slut."

Carrie Anne blinked. "A slut?"

"Well, look at you. You're like half-naked."

"You sound like my dad now."

"Speaking of your dad, what will he think of that dress?"

Carrie Anne frowned.

"I'm not trying to be mean," Sophie said. "But you guys are all sending mixed messages here."

"Mixed messages?" Kelsey tugged the bodice of her skimpy dress a little higher. "How so?"

"You know what I'm talking about." Now Sophie wished she'd never opened her big mouth. Who was she to talk anyway?

"I know what she means," Hannah said quietly. "We've all made the purity pledge, and here we—"

"Except me," Jenny chimed in.

"Yes, except you."

"Although, just for the record, I am still a virgin and I do not plan on having sex anytime soon." Jenny smiled smugly.

"Thanks for the news flash," Carrie Anne said.

"But Sophie's actually making a good point," Hannah continued. "And what about what Jeanette and Phil told us at youth group last week? What about making a promise with our lips and not with our hearts?"

"They said that?" Sophie waited to hear more.

"Phil said that it's better not to make a promise than to make a promise and break it." Jenny nodded. "See, he's helping to support my theory."

"And if we really are serious about our purity pledge . . ." Hannah turned around and looked at herself in the big three-way mirror. Her hot pink strapless dress was so tight that Sophie wondered how she could possibly breathe, let alone sit down in a chair or eat. "Why are we dressing like this?"

"So what are you suggesting we do?" Kelsey directed this to Sophie. "Should we all go to the dance wearing baggy turtle-neck dresses that cover every square inch of flesh?"

Sophie shook her head. "I probably shouldn't have said anything. Just forget—"

"No," Jenny said firmly. "I think you're right, Sophie. We do need to tone it down a little."

"Yeah." Carrie Anne said. "My dad would probably have a cow if he saw me in this dress."

Kelsey frowned at her own image in the mirror. Her formal was a sparkly turquoise number but cut so low in the back that Sophie thought Kelsey might have a serious problem if she actually attempted to dance in it. "But I like this dress. It brings out the color in my eyes."

"Check out the back side," Hannah said as she spun her around.

Jenny reached over and tugged the dress down another inch. "I can see your underwear, Kelsey."

"Hey!" Kelsey smacked Jenny's hand. "Watch it."

"Well, would you rather reveal your behind to us or to everyone at the dance?"

"Or to your parents?" Hannah challenged.

The girls continued to argue, but Sophie managed to stay out of it. Finally, as they were bickering about which was worse—showing too much cleavage or too much back—Sophie slipped back into her changing room and got dressed in her own clothes. She was sick of trying things on. Something about a pregnant girl shopping for a formal gown and lecturing her friends about purity promises was just way too creepy.

As it turned out, Mr. Young was right. The more distracted Sophie became with her new role as chief editor, the less she obsessed over other troubles. This was the first year the school had done both an online daily newspaper as well as the bimonthly printed one. Keeping up was a challenge.

"It's almost like a full-time job," she admitted to Wes as they put the paper to bed on Friday afternoon.

"But this experience is going to look really great on the college apps." Wes turned off his computer. "Have you started applying yet?"

She shook her head.

"Well, you don't want to put it off too long."

"No . . ." She reached for her bag.

"So, are you going to the big game tonight?"

"As much as I'd like to just go home and sleep for a couple of days, I promised Carrie Anne I'd go with her."

Wes grinned. "Great. See ya there then."

She nodded, feigning a smile. "Yeah."

"And, uh, my mom told me to ask you what color your dress is . . . you know, for tomorrow night's dance."

"Black."

"Black?" His tone was curious.

"Yeah. You have a problem with black?" She was ready to lay into him if he did. She'd already taken enough grief from her friends about her choice of color. They were all going with tropical shades and felt like she was the spoiler for choosing black. But her mom had helped her find a dress that Sophie felt was appropriate. Well, for a pregnant girl anyway.

Wes held up his hands defensively. "Black is good."

"Good."

"So, I'll see you at the game then." He grabbed up his laptop case and hurried out of the journalism room.

"All finished?" Mr. Young asked as he locked his office door.

"Yep." Sophie nodded.

"And you're still glad you're chief editor?"

"Well, it's keeping me busy."

He chuckled as he gathered up his briefcase and things. "And out of trouble?"

She rolled her eyes. "Yeah, right."

"Have a good weekend. I'm sure you'll be busy with all the homecoming activities."

"Yeah, pretty much." She didn't bother to tell him that she wasn't looking forward to all the activities or that she'd rather just take a long nap. Better yet, she wished she could just hibernate until, say, mid-May.

She felt even more tired that evening. Despite the fact that their team was winning—although the margin was shrinking in the second half—and the crowd was rowdy and loud and wound up, all Sophie wanted was to go home and sleep.

"Are you okay?" Wes asked. He'd invited himself to join her and her friends. Naturally she hadn't told him no. Still, she knew that some friends were beginning to think they were really a couple, which was so not the case.

"I'm fine," she snapped.

"Sorry." He looked slightly wounded.

"Sorry," she said more gently. "The truth is, I'm tired. It's been a long week and—"

"Want to make a fast break and get out of here?" he said.

"Seriously?" Sophie stood up and nudged Carrie Anne. "Wes and I are getting outta here."

"But the game's not even—"

"I know." Sophie rubbed her forehead. "But I have a headache and the noise is getting to me." Now that wasn't even a total lie.

"Okay." Carrie Anne frowned. "See ya."

As they walked across the parking lot, the night air felt cool and good against her face. "Thanks, Wes," she told him. "I really was relieved to escape. But I hope I didn't ruin your—"

"Hey, you know I'm not much of a sports fan."

"Well, I know you're not much of a sportswriter." She socked him in the arm.

"Thanks a lot."

As they got into his car, Wes asked if she was hungry. The truth was, she was hungry. But she told him no thanks and that she mostly wanted to get home. Fortunately he didn't seem to mind.

"Thanks again," she said as he pulled into her driveway. "And I'll see you at Carrie Anne's tomorrow night. It sounds like her mom's got something really great for dinner."

"Cool." He smiled at her. "Can't wait."

She nodded and tried to look enthusiastic. Really, shouldn't this be a fun time for her? Shouldn't she be enjoying all this senior year stuff?

As she went into the house, she reminded herself that she wasn't the only pregnant girl in their high school. Of course, the pregnant girls she'd noticed weren't like her—not honor students, newspaper editors, or Christians who'd made abstinence pledges. As far as Sophie knew, the girls who walked around school with their pregnant bellies hanging out were known for sleeping around. They were the kind of girls you expected to get knocked up. And they acted totally nonchalant about it, strutting around in maternity wear like they were setting a new fashion trend.

Somehow Sophie knew she just couldn't do that. As much as she liked making jokes at her own expense, she couldn't bear to have her peers laughing at her—the way she'd seen them laugh at others—just because she was pregnant. So not funny.

11

"You look hot," Carrie Anne told Sophie the following night. The two of them were dressed for the dance and standing in front of Carrie Anne's mirror doing their final tweaks. They'd already spent the afternoon helping Mrs. Vincent with the dinner preparations, trying to make everything perfect, until she had finally shooed them away to get dressed.

Sophie studied herself in the mirror and had to concede with her friend. She did look unusually good in the simple black dress. "I was worried that it might look too boring," she admitted. "But Mom talked me into it. She was so convinced it was perfect that she even paid for it too."

"Well, it's definitely hot." Carrie Anne added another bobby pin to secure Sophie's pinned-up hair. "And slimming too."

Sophie's hand automatically slid down to her midsection. Sure, she wasn't really showing, but suddenly she was reminded of what was going on inside her body. It was funny how sometimes, even if only briefly, she would forget about it. She would be tricked into thinking she was just the same as ever. Just Sophie Ramsay enjoying being a normal teenage girl. Then something would happen or someone would say something . . . and she would remember.

Fortunately the dinner and dance proved to be fairly good distractions. Although Sophie wasn't enjoying herself as much as she portrayed, it wasn't as bad as she'd expected either. Still, she was glad when it was over with. It seemed that was all she lived for anymore—getting things over with.

"Thanks for going with me tonight," Wes told her as he walked her to her door. Carrie Anne and Drew were still in the car, and suddenly Sophie felt nervous. She so hoped that Wes wasn't going to ruin what had been a sort of okay evening by trying to get a good-night kiss.

"Thank you," she told him, extending her hand as if to shake his.

He took her hand and made a goofy grin. "Good night."

"Good night." Then she pulled her hand away from his and hurried inside her house. Awkward moment averted.

As exhausted as Sophie felt, she was wide-awake when she finally got into bed. She felt restless and edgy and uneasy. Like something was about to happen.

Suddenly it occurred to her that her body could be telling her something. Like maybe something was wrong with the pregnancy. Like maybe she was going to have a miscarriage. On one hand, it would be such a relief. On the other hand, she knew it was wrong to wish for an innocent baby's death simply to escape her own mistake.

Even so, she'd already done some research about this on-line. She had actually hoped to discover some simple solution to ending the pregnancy without having an abortion. Of course, she felt guilty at the hope she'd experienced when she discovered that miscarriages were fairly common, at least statistically. But her research hadn't revealed anything terribly helpful. It seemed most miscarriages had to do with serious illnesses or DNA problems or aging. None of which seemed applicable to Sophie. She also learned that things like exercise, foods, or even sex do not cause miscarriage. Not that she was considering sex. But she had been open to a strenuous workout regime or eating weird foods—though now those things seemed pointless.

Sophie got up and turned on her computer. Once again she was surfing the Internet looking for information about miscarriages. Finally she found an article that gave her a smidgeon of hope. It seemed that stress could actually cause a miscarriage. Well, who was more stressed than Sophie? That had to be her answer. She read on to discover that her stressed-out body was quite possibly producing a hormone that could put her pregnancy at serious risk. She exited the site, removed it from her file history, and shut down the computer.

Could that be what was happening to her? Was it possible that her body was taking care of this problem itself? She had read that one in eight pregnancies miscarried in the first trimester—and she had hoped that she would be that lucky one. She was still in her first trimester and would be for at least one more month.

If Sophie was still on speaking terms with God, she might've asked for his help in this. But, on second thought, God probably wasn't inclined to listen to prayers from pregnant teenage girls who had broken their vows and were now desperately begging him to straighten things out. Or worse yet, who were hoping that a human life might end simply for convenience's sake. No, that didn't make much sense. As far as she knew, God didn't work like that. But perhaps her own body would help her out of this mess. Because one thing she knew for sure, she was totally stressed. As weird as it seemed, maybe stress would be her new best friend.

Sophie felt a tiny ray of hope as she got back into bed. Who knew that stress could actually be good for something?

Although Sophie's stress level felt higher than ever, sometimes so much so that she worried she was about to have a nervous breakdown, the next few weeks passed without the slightest sign of a miscarriage.

"So what are you kids doing for Halloween this year?" Dad asked her one night when her family of three actually sat down to eat a take-out pizza together.

"Oh, I thought I'd dress up like a pumpkin and go trick-or-treating," she said sarcastically. "I'm like almost eighteen, Dad."

"You keep pigging out on that pizza, and all you'll need is to borrow my orange T-shirt to pass yourself off as the Great Pumpkin," her dad teased.

She set down the piece and frowned. "Thanks a lot."

"Lighten up, Bud," her mom warned him. "Your waistline isn't anything to brag about."

"You making fun of my little old beer belly?" He winked at Mom. "And here I thought you liked it."

"I'm just saying . . . The truth is, I think we could all use to take off a few pounds," she said. "Maybe we should make a goal to cut back before the holidays hit and we all overdo it."

"And maybe I should sign us all up for one of those reality shows," he shot back at her. "You know, like *The Biggest Loser*. Only we could do one for families."

"Count me out." Sophie pushed back her chair and stood.

"Aw, come on," Dad said. "I was just kidding about the pumpkin thing. Finish your pizza, honey."

"I'm full."

"See what you did, Bud?" Mom shook her finger at him.

"I didn't mean anything by—"

"Seriously." Sophie faked a smile in hopes that her parents wouldn't get into some big stupid fight over her now. "I *am* full."

She went upstairs to her room, shut the door, went over to the mirror, and pulled up her shirt to stare at her rounded tummy. Her favorite jeans were too tight now, and even her usually loose khakis had gotten snug. According to what she'd read, she shouldn't require real maternity clothes until her second trimester. But that was just around the corner now. In the meantime, she couldn't go around busting out of her clothes. If her dad was noticing her weight gain, surely others would too.

Once again she went online, this time to a maternity clothes site. But everything she saw there seemed to only accentuate the pregnancy. What was up with these women showing off their bulging bellies? What she needed was a disguise. Baggy sweats seemed to be her best bet. And if her friends assumed she was simply putting on weight, so be it. That was preferable to the truth. Right now she couldn't face the truth herself. How could she expect anyone else to?

She let out a long, exasperated sigh. Why was it that some women (ones who really wanted babies) experienced miscarriages, and others didn't? What was fair about that? If God was truly the Creator like she believed—if he was the giver of life—why had Sophie wound up with this unwanted pregnancy, while other women who longed for children would never have any? And what about those who were grieving for babies they'd lost? How was that even close to fair?

Sometimes Sophie wondered how God could even sleep at night. Okay, she knew that he never actually slept at all. But how did he justify all of this?

Really, if God was as smart as she thought he was supposed to be, why had he designed females to be capable of reproduction while they were still teenagers? Seriously, what teenager was responsible enough to have and raise a child? Not her. And she was actually fairly mature for her age. Or so she used to think. But as she considered the other girls in her school—the ones who wore pregnancy like a badge—she only felt more confused.

Not that she had time to think about all those things just now. She had an op-ed piece due tomorrow and no idea of what to write about. She'd already covered most of her favorite hot topics.

Then it hit her. Why not write about teen pregnancy? She certainly had some opinions about that!

So she did. She wrote and rewrote and finally thought she'd said what she wanted to say: teens should not be sexually active because it could result in unwanted pregnancies, and teens were *not* mature enough to be parents. She didn't spare anyone's feelings in the piece. Good grief, she was lecturing herself as much as anyone.

But the next day, when it was time to hand her piece over to Mr. Young, Sophie felt unsure. Maybe she'd overstated it a bit. Been a little vehement.

"Are you giving that to me or not?"

"Oh." She frowned down at the paper in her hand. "Yeah, I guess."

"Sounds like you're not too sure of yourself, Sophie."

She just shrugged, then turned and went to her workstation. Soon she was lost in editing a poorly written assignment that Justina had turned in late.

"Interesting piece, Sophie," Mr. Young said.

"What?" Sophie looked up from her computer screen.

"Your op-ed." He shook his head. "Too bad you didn't have much of an opinion on that one."

"I didn't?" She blinked.

"I'm kidding. You expressed yourself quite well."

"Oh."

"But you could take some flak with that one."

"And is that supposed to make me back down from my opinion?"

He grinned. "No way. You're chief editor, Sophie. Your job is to call it like you see it. Controversy is what makes an editorial section interesting and outstanding. I hope we get some responses on this one."

"Okay." She nodded with satisfaction.

As it turned out, they did get some responses to it. It seemed that Sophie had hit a nerve with a number of people. Including Mrs. Manchester, the woman who headed up the teen pregnancy center at school.

"I'd like to meet whoever wrote this piece," she told Mr. Young the day after the paper came out.

"Certainly." He motioned Sophie over and quickly introduced them.

"Well." Mrs. Manchester just shook her head. "It's clear that you have no idea what you're writing about, young lady."

"What?" Sophie frowned at her, then turned to Mr. Young for support.

"Feel free to use my office to discuss this if you'd like," he told them.

"Actually . . ." Sophie glanced back to her workstation. "I have work to do here, Mrs. Manchester. If you have an opinion to express, I suggest you write a letter to the editor. We'll be happy to print it in our next edition."

Mrs. Manchester looked like she was about to sputter. "Yes, I can certainly do that. Since it's obvious that you've given very little serious thought to what you chose to write about."

Sophie narrowed her eyes at the woman. "How do you know that?"

"You're so judgmental. You come across as Miss Know-It-All, but I suspect you're clueless when it comes to how it feels to be a pregnant teen. You wrote as if you thought girls get pregnant on purpose. Or as if they have no regrets. Clearly you don't know what you're talking about. I doubt that any of your friends are pregnant. Are they?"

"Well, not that I know of."

"See. My point."

Sophie frowned.

"If you want to be better informed, I suggest you come down to the pregnancy center and spend some time with my girls. Get to know them and get to understand their problems and challenges before you go spouting off your opinions about who they are and how they got there."

"Well, I don't—"

"Just as I thought. You don't care enough about them to actually get involved. You just decided to take potshots from the comfort of your editor's chair."

"That's not true."

The woman's brows arched. "Really?"

Now Sophie wanted to sputter.

"I intend to write a letter to rebut your claims, Miss Ramsay. You can count on it."

Sophie gave her a stiff smile. "And if your invitation is sincere, I'll come and visit your center and speak to some of the girls there."

Mrs. Manchester softened ever so slightly. "Perhaps when you see they are human and have feelings, you'll want to write another piece."

"Perhaps." Sophie stood up straighter. "Now, if you'll excuse me, I have work to do."

"Yes, I'm sure we all do." Mrs. Manchester turned and left the room.

Wes joined Sophie. "Looks like you poked the hornet's nest with that one."

"Apparently so."

"Everything okay?" Mr. Young asked. "Mrs. Manchester seemed a little upset."

"Ya think?" Sophie just shook her head. "She wants me to come and spend time with her girls now."

"Hey, that's a great idea. Maybe you could do a human interest piece. I'm sure that most kids don't know what goes on in the pregnancy center."

"I'm sure most of them don't *want* to know either." Sophie made a face.

"I don't know what goes on there." Wes looked slightly intrigued. "But I think it could be interesting."

"See?" Mr. Young nodded. "Inquiring minds want to know."

"Yeah, and it's probably just the kind of story that would fit in the *National Enquirer* too."

Just the same, Sophie decided to follow this up. After her last class, she walked across campus to a separate building where the teen pregnancy center was located. It was a modular structure, cheap and slightly temporary looking—and not a place that a girl like Sophie really wanted to be seen going into. But, she reminded herself, this was research.

"Can I help you?" asked a young woman who was sitting in what appeared to be a reception area.

"Mrs. Manchester told me that I could come here and check things out." Sophie smiled.

"Oh, I see." The young woman's eyes looked sympathetic. "When are you due?"

Sophie blinked. "What?"

"Aren't you here to sign up for the program?"

"The program?" Sophie felt like running away.

"You're not pregnant?" The woman seemed confused.

"Sophie Ramsay," Mrs. Manchester said as she came into the reception area. Then she laughed. "No, Lisa, Sophie is not pregnant. She's the one who wrote that nasty editorial."

"Oh." Lisa scowled at Sophie. "That wasn't very nice."

"Sorry. But it was an opinion piece."

"And she certainly has her opinions." Mrs. Manchester tossed Lisa a knowing glance. "But perhaps we can change some of her views. I assume you came to talk to some of the girls here, Sophie?"

"I'm researching a human interest story," Sophie said. "If it's okay, I've got a recorder for interviews and a camera to take some shots." She pulled out some release forms. "But you'll have to get these signed for permission. Do you think this is a good time?"

"I think we can accommodate you." She put a hand on Sophie's shoulder. "Why don't you sit in on this next class, and when it's break time, I'll introduce you and we'll see if any of the girls would like to talk to you."

"Sounds good."

"It's a child development class and a requirement for all the mothers-to-be." Mrs. Manchester put her forefinger over her lips, then opened the door, nodding to a seat in the back.

Sophie noticed the glances that were shot her way. Some were suspicious. Others were amused. They probably thought she was one of them. In reality, she was. Not that she intended to tip that hand.

Instead she took out her laptop and proceeded to take notes, at the same time discreetly observing the students in the class. The girls appeared to be of varying ethnicities, socioeconomic levels, and stages of pregnancy—well, except for the one with an infant in her arms. What surprised Sophie most was the number of girls present—thirteen! If anyone had asked, she would've guessed that only about four or five pregnant girls attended her school. It seemed she was wrong. Wrong about a lot of things.

As the teacher discussed the basics of infant nutrition, including the benefits of breast-fed babies compared to formula-fed ones, Sophie could see a diverse reaction among the girls. A few nodded with interest as they took notes, like they were trying to absorb the information. A number of others had blank stares, like they wanted to be anywhere else but here right now. But a couple of the girls looked seriously frightened. Sophie could relate to them best.

After the class ended, Mrs. Manchester returned and introduced Sophie as the editor who'd done the teen pregnancy piece. Naturally this brought some pretty dark looks from the girls.

"I'm here to find out what's really going on," Sophie said. "I realize that I was writing out of ignorance and opinion. But my goal is to get to the truth. I hope you'll help me to do that."

"Not if you plan on printing our names." A blond girl scowled at her.

"That's Serena," Mrs. Manchester told Sophie. "And she makes a good point. Some girls may prefer anonymity."

"I can do that," Sophie told them. "I just want for other students to understand how you're feeling, what you're going through, and why the pregnancy center is needed . . . if it is needed."

Well, that got the discussion started. It's like Sophie had tripped the trigger, and now these girls were ready to tear into Sophie like she was the enemy—like they might lash out at some of Sophie's opinionated friends if they had the guts to come here and spout their views.

To be honest, Sophie thought she probably deserved this.

12

"What's up with you being spotted at the pregnancy center yesterday?" Carrie Anne asked Sophie at lunch.

"Who spotted me there?" Sophie kept her voice level, but she could feel her heart rate increasing. Hopefully no one was getting the wrong idea about her. Well, maybe it was the right idea, but Sophie wasn't ready to face it yet.

"Drew said he saw you coming out of the building when he was on his way to soccer practice. He asked me why you were hanging with pregnant chicks."

"What *were* you doing there?" Kelsey stared at Sophie in horror.

"Does this have anything to do with that scathing editorial you wrote?" Jenny asked. "Man, I'm surprised those girls would let you near the pregnancy center after the way you made them sound like total idiots."

"They *are* total idiots," Kelsey said.

"I did *not* make them sound like idiots," Sophie protested. "I just wanted to make the point that kids should not be raising kids."

"You're right about that," Hannah said. "And I think the school is just encouraging it by offering the pregnancy center. It's like they're saying, 'It's okay, go ahead and get knocked up. We'll take care of you and your baby.'"

"I agree," Kelsey piped in. "It's like these girls get a false sense of security, like everything's just fine, and decide it's cool to keep their babies."

"Well, maybe it is all right for some girls to keep their babies," Jenny said. "I mean, who died and made you God?"

"I'm not saying I'm God." Kelsey glared at her. "I'm just saying if a girl is dumb enough to get knocked up, she should be smart enough to know she's too dumb to raise a kid."

"Like that's supposed to make sense?" Jenny rolled her eyes.

"Look, we don't have to fight about it." Sophie held up her hands. "Everyone is entitled to their opinion, right?"

"Well, some people might take exception to that particular opinion." Jenny pointed to herself. "For instance, my mom was only eighteen when she had me. And I don't think she's doing too bad a job of it."

"Seriously?" Sophie said. "I knew your mom was kind of young, but I had no idea."

"Yeah, it's not the kind of thing a girl likes to brag about."

"Well, that was a long time ago," Kelsey protested. "People should be smarter now. Don'tcha think?"

"Especially with all the abstinence campaigns going on," Hannah added.

"Like that's gonna solve the problem." Jenny's tone was sarcastic. "Girls still get pregnant."

"Not this girl." Hannah shook her head vigorously.

"Or this one." Kelsey made a face. "Ugh, can you imagine how totally humiliating it would be to have to take classes at the pregnancy center?"

Carrie Anne nodded. "Seriously, Sophie, what were you doing there anyway? I mean, you already wrote your little opinion piece."

"I'm doing a human interest story for the paper."

"Good for you," Jenny said.

"Well . . . I guess it's something people need to know about. I had no idea there were so many girls there."

"How many are there?"

"They told me it's around thirty. But they're not all from Brewster. Some of the girls come over from Maxwell too. Some are pregnant, and some already have a kid. Some do half days and some do whole days."

"So they bring their kids to school with them?"

Sophie nodded. "There's a pretty nice day-care facility and everything. It's quite an operation."

"Isn't it freaky, though, Sophie?" Kelsey asked. "I mean, didn't it feel weird being there with all those pregnant girls? Didn't you want to just tell them that they wouldn't be in that place if they'd just waited until their wedding night to—"

"Yeah, that'd be real nice." Jenny punched Kelsey in the arm.

"Ouch!"

"Just because a girl makes a stupid mistake doesn't mean she doesn't have feelings too. Sheesh."

"Are you speaking from experience?" Kelsey narrowed her eyes at Jenny.

"Yeah, right. I'm pregnant, Kelsey. Get real."

"Well, you're the only one in our group who hasn't made a purity pledge."

"Puhleeze, don't remind me."

"Jenny's right, though," Sophie admitted.

"Right about what?" Kelsey asked. "Not making a pledge?"

"No. She's right that those girls *do* have feelings."

"And aren't we supposed to love everyone?" Jenny asked.

"It's not that I *don't* love them exactly." Kelsey spoke slowly like she was trying to figure it out. "It's just that I don't want to be *seen* with them. You guys know that we're not supposed to put on an appearance of evil. I mean, if I was *with* girls like that, someone might think that I'm like that too."

A small part of Sophie wanted to scream out to Kelsey and the whole world that she herself was a girl like that. But she kept quiet.

"Well, I think you're full of it," Jenny said to Kelsey. "And just for the record, Jesus hung with people who were considered evil and sinful. I think it's cool that Sophie doesn't mind hanging with the pregnant girls. You go, Sophie."

Sophie let out an exasperated sigh. If only they knew.

"I agree with Jenny." Carrie Anne patted Sophie on the back. "You go, girl."

"You must be better Christians than me." Kelsey's voice was too loud. "Trust me, if I had to spend time with a bunch of dumb pregnant teen girls, I'd want to straighten them all out."

"I know what my dad would say." Carrie Anne's voice softened. "Actually, it's what Jesus said."

"What?" Kelsey said.

"You know . . . that whoever is without sin should throw the first stone."

"Thank God I'm without *that* sin," Kelsey said.

Their group erupted into laughter. Well, Jenny didn't laugh all that much, and Sophie's laugh sounded fake to her own ears. For the most part, her friends just didn't really get it. And Sophie wasn't much closer to getting it than they were. The truth was, she *was* embarrassed to be seen hanging with the pregnant girls. Never mind that she was actually one of them.

Consequently, she glanced over her shoulder as she made her way to the pregnancy center that afternoon. She didn't really want to be spotted again, despite the fact that she was on an assignment and had arranged to do three interviews. She still felt uneasy as she went into the center.

Music was playing, and the place was decorated with black and orange streamers. Cutouts of pumpkins, cats, witches, and ghosts were plastered here and there. Mrs. Manchester had told Sophie that some of the teen moms were having a

Halloween party for their babies. Why babies needed a Halloween party was a mystery to Sophie. But maybe it was for the moms. Anyway, it provided a good opportunity for Sophie to get her interviews done.

"You're back," Serena said.

Sophie nodded. "We have an appointment, remember?"

"I remember. But I figured you might just forget. Most kids try to avoid this place like they think we have some disease that's catching."

"Is that really how you feel?" Sophie turned on the mini recorder as they sat down in Mrs. Manchester's office.

"It's how we all feel. Like we have the plague or something." She rubbed her oversized stomach, then shook her head. "I promise you it's not contagious. But you do catch it from a boy." She laughed.

"Right."

"I don't see what the big deal is, really. I mean, you sleep with a guy and you get pregnant. I guess it's just a problem because I'm still in high school."

"Do you plan to graduate?"

Serena frowned. "I don't know for sure."

"What year are you?"

"Just a sophomore."

Sophie tried not to act shocked. "Oh."

"I know, I know. It sounds hopeless. My mama is furious at me for doing this to her."

"To her?"

"Well, yeah, that's how she puts it. Like I went and got myself knocked up just to punish her or something. It wasn't like that."

"No, I didn't think so."

"Anyway, she keeps telling me that I got no business wanting to keep my baby when I don't even have a high school diploma. Like she thinks she's going to have to support me and my son for the rest of her life."

"Your son?"

"Yeah. It's a boy. I told his daddy that I have a feeling he's gonna look just like him." She pulled up her shirt to show off an enormous belly. "See how big I am? His daddy is six foot four. You know Reggie Grant, the senior, varsity basketball?"

"He's your boyfriend?"

"Well, he ain't my boyfriend no more."

"You broke up?"

"Yeah, you could say that."

"What happened?"

"He dumped me." She shook her head. "As soon as he heard I was pregnant, he went running the other way."

"Sorry."

"Yeah . . . me too." To Sophie's relief, Serena pulled her shirt back down. "Now he's dating Chelsea Walters."

"That must be rough."

"Yeah . . . but I probably don't want to go there right now. Not with that thing on anyway." She nodded toward the recorder. "By the way, Mrs. Manchester said you could use fake names in your article."

"You want me to do that?"

"Yeah. Please."

Sophie asked about a dozen more questions and finally thanked Serena for her honesty.

"You won't make me sound like an idiot, will you?"

"That's not my goal. But I do want to write this honestly. I mean, it's possible that some girl might learn something by reading your story."

"Like not to let her boyfriend pressure her into sex?"

"Yeah."

"And to use protection if he does?"

Sophie just nodded. She wasn't sure she wanted to go there.

Serena stood and rubbed her back. "Want me to send in the next girl?"

"Thanks." Sophie looked down at her notes. "Natasha Lebkowski."

"Oh yeah. That Natasha gal. She's a real piece of work."

"You don't like her?"

"She don't give anyone the chance to like her."

"Oh."

When Natasha came into the room, Sophie knew this girl had a serious attitude. Her long, dark hair was pulled back in a tight ponytail, and her face, while pretty, looked strained and angry. Sophie introduced herself and extended her hand.

But Natasha ignored the gesture. Instead, she sat down, folded her arms over her rounded midsection, and just glared at Sophie.

"So . . ." Sophie began carefully, "you seem unhappy."

"You got that right."

"Any particular reason?"

"I'm looking at her."

Sophie blinked. "I'm surprised you agreed to be interviewed then."

"I agreed to be interviewed for one reason."

"And that is?"

"To set you straight."

"Okay." Sophie nodded. "Go for it."

"You don't know me."

"That's true."

"And yet you feel qualified to write about me—about girls like me—as if you know what we're going through and how we got to this place. You point your finger and pass your judgments, and your head is up your—"

"Look, I'm sorry I wrote that opinion piece, okay?"

"Sure, you can say that now. But isn't that kind of like pulling the trigger and then saying, 'Oops, I'm sorry'? Some bullets can't be retracted."

Sophie nodded. "You're right."

"Do you honestly think I made the choice to be here? To be pregnant? To be humiliated by girls like you? To be stuck in this—"

"Just a minute." Sophie held up a finger. "Are you saying you didn't make the choice to have sex? Like this is some kind of immaculate conception or virgin birth?" The truth was, Sophie wished she could use that excuse for herself.

"No, you moron." Natasha narrowed her dark eyes. "It's not immaculate conception. But I wouldn't be surprised if that's what you decide to write in your stupid article. Might get a laugh too. Kids like to laugh at us. Don't think we don't hear it."

"I'm sure you do hear it." Sophie felt like her head was spinning. Natasha was smart. Almost too smart. And she was saying just the kinds of things that Sophie didn't really want to hear.

"You asked me about choice," Natasha continued. "Well, sometimes it's not about choice. Have you ever heard of date rape?"

Sophie tried not to look shocked. "Is that what happened?"

"Yes." Natasha nodded.

"Did you press charges?"

Natasha just looked away.

"Did you?"

"No, of course not. I'm not a fool."

"But why? Why didn't you?"

"Do you have any idea what happens when you press charges for date rape?"

Sophie considered this. "I suppose I can imagine."

"Well, imagine this. The boy is a friend of my parents. His dad plays golf with my dad. He's in an Ivy League school. It's his word against mine."

Sophie leaned forward. "So what's he doing about it now? Is he taking responsibility for—"

"Oh, sure. His parents are paying the bills. Terrence admitted that we'd had sex. Of course, he made it look like I had seduced him!" She swore.

"I'm sorry."

"Well, don't be," she snapped. "Be glad."

"Glad?"

"That you're not me. That you still have your life ahead of you."

Suddenly Sophie felt like she couldn't get her breath, like the room was beginning to spin. She closed her eyes and tried to think. Why had she come here? Why was she talking to this girl? Was she just a glutton for punishment or what?

"Are you okay?"

Sophie opened her eyes to see Natasha staring at her with concern. "Sorry."

"Are you sick or something?"

"I just got dizzy."

"Maybe it's low blood sugar." Natasha reached for her bag. Sophie wasn't an expert, but it looked like an expensive bag. In fact, everything about Natasha, despite her simple clothing, seemed to suggest this girl came from money. Natasha pulled out a bag of hard caramels and handed it to Sophie. "I get it sometimes. This helps."

Sophie nodded as she unwrapped the candy and popped it in her mouth.

"We can end this interview now," Natasha said. "If you want."

"Can I ask a few more questions?"

"If you can take the answers."

"Well, this isn't a hard one. You don't seem familiar."

"That's because I went to Maxwell. They don't have a pregnancy center there. Not that they don't need one."

"But they act like they don't?"

"Bingo." She kind of laughed. "They send their *disappointments* to Brewster. It keeps Maxwell looking good."

"So, did you consider having an abortion?"

"Oh yeah."

"And?"

"I couldn't do it."

"Is it for religious reasons?"

"Nope."

"Do you mind saying why? I mean, some pro-life people use rape as one of the justifiable reasons for abortion."

"I'm aware of that."

"So . . . ?"

"The truth is, I didn't think I was pregnant at first. It seemed impossible. I mean, who gets pregnant on their first time?"

"It was your first time?"

Natasha looked down at her lap and nodded.

"How old are you?"

"Sixteen."

"Oh . . . Okay, so you considered abortion but decided against it?"

She nodded again. "If I had known that there was any chance I was pregnant, I would've gotten that next-day pill."

"If you'd reported the rape, they probably would've given it to you."

"I know."

"So, are you sorry you didn't report the crime and go in for an examination . . . and the next-day pill?"

"Sure. I'm sorry I went out with Terrence too. I'm sorry for a lot of things."

"So . . . what will happen after the birth of your baby?"

"You mean, am I keeping the baby?"

"Yes."

"Probably not."

"Probably?"

"Well, my mom is being very weird about the whole thing."

"How so?"

"Naturally she was really upset. Like, how could I do this to her?"

"Did you tell her the truth? I mean, about the date rape?"

"No."

"Why not?"

"What would be the point?"

"I don't know," Sophie admitted.

"So, after my mom recovered from the shock—by the way, my dad is still not speaking to me."

"That's too bad."

"Yeah, Daddy's girl let him down."

"I understand."

"Sure you do." Natasha narrowed her eyes with skepticism. "But anyway, once Mom got over it, she started to get this whacked-out idea that Terrence and I would get married eventually. And in the meantime, she's acting like she's going to be the happy grandma."

"Oh, wow."

"Yeah. Wow."

"So how do you feel about it?"

"I think I'll let the baby be adopted."

"And your mom?"

"She'll probably be ticked."

"Pregnancy really messes up your life."

Natasha laughed with sarcasm. "Tell me something I don't know."

Sophie was tempted tell her everything. But she didn't. Instead she just asked a few more questions, thanked her, and then interviewed the last girl. Her name was Leah, and her story was different from the other two. She was a quiet senior who was still with her boyfriend. He had graduated last year and was working in a factory. They were going to get married at Christmas, and they would keep their child and "live happily ever after."

"That seems a lot to take on," Sophie said finally.

"It's not that big of a deal," Leah assured Sophie. "We knew we wanted to get married. It's just a little earlier than we'd planned."

"It won't be easy."

"What is?"

Sophie considered this as she walked to her car. What was easy? She couldn't even remember.

13

"What do you mean you're not coming tonight?" Carrie Anne's brow creased.

"I mean I'm not coming." Sophie unlocked her car, threw in her bag, then turned to face her friend.

"But you *always* come to the church harvest party."

They'd met in the school parking lot. Because of the interviews, Sophie had gotten out of school the same time as the rest of the students. But now she was tired, and since there wasn't yearbook on Fridays, she just wanted to go home and sleep.

"It's been a long day," Sophie told Carrie Anne.

"Are you coming with us, Carrie Anne?" Kelsey called.

"I guess so." Carrie Anne frowned at Sophie. "Since my best friend is such a party pooper."

"Sorry."

Carrie Anne stared at Sophie with a serious expression. "You're changing, you know?"

Sophie felt a jolt of fear rush through her. What was Carrie Anne saying? "What do you mean?"

"I mean you're different." Carrie Anne continued to stare.

"Because I don't want to go to the kiddy party at church?"

"See?" Carrie Anne pointed a finger at her.

"See what?"

"You used to love the harvest party and anything that had to do with church. Now you don't. See, you've changed."

Kelsey, Jenny, and Hannah were coming toward them.

"No," Sophie said quickly, "I haven't changed. I'm just tired. Here's the deal. Let me go home and take a nap, and then I'll meet you guys at the harvest party. Okay?"

Carrie Anne didn't look convinced.

"What's up?" Jenny asked as she and the others joined them.

"Sophie needs to go home and have a wittle nappie," Carrie Anne said in a baby voice.

"Oh, poor thing," Kelsey teased. "Doing a full day at school wore you out?"

"Whatever." Sophie rolled her eyes. "I'm tired, okay?"

"Maybe you've got mono," Jenny said. "I heard it's going around."

"You have to kiss someone to get mono," Kelsey pointed out. "And that's obviously not happening to this girl."

"Thanks a lot." Sophie made a face.

"I don't know." Jenny giggled. "Wes sticks pretty close to her."

"Hey, you guys can stand here and discuss my love life, or the lack thereof, until the cows come home. In the meantime, I'm going to take a nap."

"I'll bet she does have mono," Hannah said as Sophie got into her car.

Sophie just smiled, waved, and slowly backed out of the parking lot. She could imagine what they were saying about her. Not necessarily mean things, since she was their friend and they were Christians, but she knew they talked differently about people when they weren't around to hear. She also knew that unless she wanted to get them really speculating about her, she needed to show up at the harvest party as well as the other church activities she'd been skipping out on. The problem was that it was hard to be around all that—sermons, discussions, Bible studies, prayer requests—when she felt like such a hypocrite. It wasn't that she'd totally abandoned her faith. It was simply that she and God weren't exactly on speaking terms lately.

She knew that God was gracious and loving and kind—at least, she knew this in her head. She also knew that if she confessed her sins, he would forgive her and make her clean. The problem was that he wouldn't make her unpregnant. He wouldn't undo what she had done. And she knew that if she took these steps with God, she would probably have to take them with her family and friends too. That was usually how it worked. Christians were supposed to confess their sins not only to God but to each other. And she just couldn't do that.

Still, she decided as she went into her house, she needed to do a better job of playing that part—the role of the good Christian girl. And if that meant putting on some lame costume and going to the harvest party and yukking it up with her friends, so be it. But first she was taking a nap!

❀

"You're home early," Sophie said to her dad as he came into the house and tossed his Carhartt jacket over a kitchen chair.

"It's a holiday."

"It's *Halloween*, Dad." She grabbed her bag.

"Halloween happens to be one of my favorite holidays."

"Well, the candy's there, what's left of it anyway." She pointed to the big bowl that everyone had been sneaking from. "We've already had some early birds. Mom will be home by six. And she's got some more candy."

"Hey, looks like you took my advice." He chuckled as he set his thermos in the sink.

"Huh?" She fished her car keys from her bag.

He poked her in the tummy and grinned. "Putting on a little weight there, aren't you, pumpkin?"

"Very funny." She looked down at the orange T-shirt she'd borrowed from his closet. She'd used black electrical tape to make a smiley face. Then she'd put it on and stuffed it full of wadded-up newspaper to resemble a lumpy jack-o'-lantern.

By the time she reached the church, the parking lot was full and the party was in full gear. She went inside, pushed past moms and kids in costume, and finally located her friends in the snack area.

"Wow, you went all out with your costume this year," Kelsey said sarcastically. She was dressed like a princess, the same costume she'd worn for the past couple of years—in Sophie's opinion, boring.

"You have something against pumpkins?"

"I'm just glad you made it." Carrie Anne gave her a sideways hug.

"What are you?" Sophie studied her black head-to-toe attire.

"A cat, of course." Carrie Anne waved her tail under Sophie's nose.

Sophie dug a green stocking hat from her bag and pulled it on her head. "Almost forgot my stem."

"Now there's a good look," Jenny teased.

"Are you supposed to be an elf or something?" Sophie asked.

"Peter Pan." Jenny bowed, then pointed to Hannah. "And this is Tinkerbell."

"Of course." Sophie laughed at the strange apparatus of wire hangers and cloth that was attached to Hannah's back. "The wings are a dead giveaway."

And so the evening went. Sophie hung with her friends, made jokes, and played the multifaceted role of good Christian girl, class clown, and loyal friend. Hopefully she dispelled any concerns that Carrie Anne or the others had about her. Of course, the constant question was, how long could she keep this up?

✽

Sophie put a lot of time into her article about the pregnancy center. But when she finally finished it on Sunday night, it wasn't exactly what she'd expected it would be. At least it was fair, though. Mostly she didn't want to think about it anymore. And when she took it to school on Monday, she hoped she wouldn't bump into any of the girls she'd interviewed. More than that, she never wanted to see the pregnancy center again.

"You've examined both sides of this issue now," Mr. Young told Sophie at their publisher's meeting. "I recommend you run this feature on the front page in the next edition."

"I agree," Wes said.

"The *front* page?" Sophie asked. "Are you sure?"

"It's a good story, Sophie." Wes nodded. "And judging by the reactions we got from your editorial, you've hit a hot button with this whole pregnancy issue."

Mr. Young gave her back the hard copy. "I think readers will appreciate your honesty."

She cringed. *Honesty?* That made her want to laugh. Or cry.

Her only escape was to lose herself in school and journalism. So for the next couple of weeks, that's what she did. By mid-November, she realized that she was feeling fairly normal again. No more morning sickness or tender breasts or excessive tiredness. It was amazing. Almost as if the whole thing had gone away, except for the fact that none of her jeans fit her now. She'd gotten some sweats and baggy clothes to cover things up. Sure, her friends occasionally took jabs at her weight, but that seemed minor compared to reality.

However, a different kind of reality began to create itself. Sophie felt so much more like her old self, so much more normal and almost happy, that she actually began to imagine she wasn't really pregnant. She knew it was a game—or that she was being the queen of denial again. But at the moment it was working.

"My mom read your story in the *Panther Paw*," Kelsey told Sophie at lunch one day. "And she wasn't too pleased."

"Huh?" Sophie looked up from her fries.

"She thinks you're being way too soft on pregnancy."

"Soft on pregnancy?" Sophie frowned.

"What did she want Sophie to do?" Jenny demanded. "Beat on the girls who were pregnant? Like they don't have enough problems?"

"Okay, maybe I didn't say that quite right." Kelsey looked contemplative. "What my mom said was that by showing the pregnancy center the way you did, and by telling those girls' stories, it was kind of like saying it was okay."

"And your point is?" Sophie glared at Kelsey.

"I know what Kelsey is saying," Carrie Anne said. "She means it's like you were endorsing the whole thing. Like it's cool to be a pregnant teen."

"Yeah," Kelsey said. "Like that *Juno* movie. Like you're glamorizing it. That's what my mom said."

"Glamorizing it?" Sophie stared at her friends like they were aliens. "Are you guys nuts?"

"Well, it did seem like you were on their side," Hannah pointed out. "Like you thought it was great that they were in the pregnancy center."

"Well, where do you guys think those girls *should* be?" Sophie took in a deep breath. "Maybe you want them to be hidden away? Treated like they have leprosy and locked away in some dark dungeon? And forget about education, right? I mean, once a girl makes a mistake or is the victim of rape—"

"You don't know that for a fact," Kelsey said.

"Are you saying that girl lied?"

"I'm saying that if I got pregnant, I'd probably say something like that too." Kelsey sat up straighter. "Not that there's any chance of that. I'm just saying."

"You guys are living in the dark ages." Jenny shook her head. "Seriously. I thought Sophie's feature was spot-on." She reached over and gave Sophie a high five. "Way to go."

"I'm not saying we should lock the pregnant girls up," Carrie Anne protested. "Just that we shouldn't reward them, you know?"

"Yeah," Kelsey agreed. "That's exactly what my mom said."

"Reward them?" Sophie wanted to scream. "You think they feel rewarded? Do you have any idea what they're going through? Did you actually read my article? Or are you guys just so judgmental that you can't even—"

"We're not judging them, Sophie," Carrie Anne argued. "We're just saying that our society keeps lowering the standards."

"Yes!" Kelsey exclaimed. "That's what my mom said too. She said that when the school makes these pregnancy centers and sets up child care, it's like giving girls permission to have sex, get pregnant, and—"

"No one needs to give anyone permission," Sophie shot back. "It's happening, Kelsey. Maybe what those girls needed was birth control."

"Birth control?" Kelsey looked shocked.

"Seriously, Sophie." Carrie Anne shook her head like she thought Sophie had lost her mind. "This doesn't even sound like you. Are you suggesting that the school nurse should be handing out birth control pills or condoms?"

"Yeah, hasn't our town already been down that road?" Hannah said.

"Maybe we need to go down it again," Sophie snapped.

"That's exactly what my mom thinks," Kelsey shot back at her. "She's already planning a meeting at church for next Saturday."

"A meeting at church?" Sophie frowned at her. "Why?"

"To inform people about what's really going on—"

"Does she even know what's going on?" Sophie was talking so loudly that others were listening now. Not that she cared.

"She knows it's time that the church got more involved," Kelsey continued, "and she thinks that our high school is going straight to—"

"Maybe she should stop thinking so much." Sophie's hands were curled into fists. "And instead of passing judgment, maybe she should spend some time with some of these pregnant girls to find out what's really—"

"I can't believe how you're defending them," Carrie Anne said. "Like you think it's okay to get pregnant while you're still in high school."

Sophie felt ready to explode. She couldn't believe how harsh and judgmental her friends—if they were her friends—had become.

"Man, Sophie." Kelsey looked stunned. "I think journalism is messing with your head. It's like you're turning into such a liberal."

"What is that supposed to mean? Because I care about people, because I feel sorry for a girl who gets pregnant, I'm suddenly a liberal?" Sophie stood up and stared at her friends. "Fine. I'm a liberal. Whatever!"

"The next thing we know you'll be pro-abortion," Kelsey sniped.

Sophie picked up her tray, walked away from the table, and counted to ten. As she dumped her tray, she counted to ten again. Some people were such morons. Seriously, if ignorance was bliss, Kelsey North had to be the happiest girl on the planet.

"Hey, sunshine."

Sophie turned to see Wes jogging to catch her.

"What's the hurry?"

She frowned. "No hurry. I just needed to escape from my friends."

"What's up?"

As they walked to the journalism room, she poured out the whole story. Well, everything except her current condition. "Now Kelsey is calling me a liberal."

Wes kind of laughed. "Some of us take that as a compliment."

Sophie considered this. "But I always thought I was fairly conservative. I mean, my parents are Republicans. I'm a Christian and pro-life. We live in a very conservative town."

"I don't see why people have to label everything." Wes sighed. "I mean, instead of just being one thing or another, maybe we need to be better informed—and come to our own conclusions."

"Yeah." She nodded, taking this in.

"And that's exactly what you did in your feature, Sophie."

"Except that now it feels like I've rocked the boat again."

"You know what they say."

"What?"

"You know, you can please some of the people some of the time . . ."

"But not all of the people ever."

"Yeah, something like that."

"Right now it just feels like I've made all my friends mad. Well, except for Jenny." Sophie paused. "And that's funny."

"Why?"

"Because Jenny used to be the one friend I never agreed with about much of anything."

"People change."

Sophie nodded. "That's true." People did change. Sometimes more than anyone knew.

14

"Great article, Sophie!"

Sophie looked up from her current project to see that Mrs. Manchester had come into the journalism room. "Thanks," she told her.

"Thank *you*. It's a pleasure to see honest journalism. The girls in the center were pleased too. Thank you for protecting their anonymity."

"Well, I'm glad someone likes it."

Mrs. Manchester nodded in an understanding way. "You rocked the boat a little?"

"Seems like that's what I do best."

"That's because you're a real newspaperwoman." This came from Mr. Young.

"I was just telling Sophie thanks for writing that piece."

"You might not be thanking me next week."

"What happens next week?" Mrs. Manchester asked.

"Hopefully nothing." Sophie frowned.

"What do you mean?" Mr. Young seemed interested now.

"Well, I just heard that Kelsey North's mom wasn't too thrilled with my article, and now she's organizing some kind of meeting."

"For what purpose?" He waited expectantly.

"My guess is to discuss the school's pregnancy center."

Mrs. Manchester looked worried. "Oh dear."

"When is this meeting scheduled?" Mr. Young asked.

"Saturday."

"Who's invited to come?"

"I'm not sure." Sophie thought for a moment. "But it's at our church, and I'd think that anyone would be welcome."

"I wish I could be there." Mrs. Manchester sighed. "But I'll be out of town for Thanksgiving."

Mr. Young slapped his forehead. "That's right. So will I."

"Maybe we should schedule another meeting," Mrs. Manchester suggested. "A town meeting. Maybe we could have it during the following week."

"Great idea," Mr. Young said. "We could get some media coverage too."

The next thing Sophie knew, they were planning a meeting and she was agreeing to participate. Great, what would her friends think of her now?

❀

"It was so nice of the Vincents to invite us for Thanksgiving," Mom said as Dad drove them across town. "It would've been lonely just the three of us this year."

"You did tell them that they have to have the TV on, didn't you?" Dad said.

"Carrie Anne knows that Bart has a ball game today," Sophie told him. "She promised that we'd watch it."

"Otherwise I'll be heading straight for home," he announced.

"I think you've already made that perfectly clear." Mom glanced back at Sophie. "Your father is such a social butterfly."

"I refuse to miss my own son's football game."

Sophie smiled. "Don't worry, Dad, Pastor Vincent likes football too."

"That's another thing," Dad growled. "Eating with church people—the pastor of the church even."

"Oh, Dad!"

"Mind your manners, Bud." Mom reached over and thumped him on the forehead.

"That means don't touch your food until Pastor Vincent is able to say a blessing," Sophie reminded him.

"And put your napkin in your lap," Mom said.

"And hold my little pinky finger when I drink my tea?" he said.

"Just be nice."

Dad parked in front of the Vincents' house, and they got out of the car. "It looks like they've got more than just us for dinner," Sophie said.

"Yes." Mom handed a casserole dish to Sophie. "Darlene said they have some good friends joining them today."

Sophie froze. "Good friends?"

"What's the matter?" her dad teased. "You're suddenly turning into a social phobic like your old man?"

"Come on, Sophie," Mom called. "I don't want those yams to get cold."

Sophie's feet felt like cement blocks as she trudged after her parents to the front door. *Please, please, please*, she actually prayed—for the first time in months—*please, please, please, God, don't let it be the Morrises. And if it is, don't let Dylan be there. Please, please, please!*

"Hey, Sophie," Carrie Anne chirped as she let Sophie and her parents into the warm house. "Guess who's here?"

Sophie felt faint. And hot. She shoved the casserole toward Carrie Anne. "This is supposed to stay warm."

"Let me take your coat, Sophie," Mrs. Vincent said.

Sophie didn't want to remove her coat, didn't want to stay, wanted to think of some excuse to dash off, but Mrs. Vincent, the consummate hostess, was already peeling it off.

"The fellows are in the den, Bud," she told Sophie's dad. "Watching football."

"I'll bet they're not drinking brewskies," he whispered to Sophie as Mrs. Vincent disappeared with their coats.

"Be good," Mom said sharply.

"Want to watch the game too?" Carrie Anne asked Sophie. "It's not your brother's game yet. But the guys are in there."

"I'll get this in the oven first." Sophie grabbed the casserole back from Carrie Anne and made a beeline for the kitchen.

"Little Susie Homemaker," Carrie Anne teased. "Meet ya in the den."

As they parted ways, Sophie knew she had to think of an excuse to leave. Maybe she could fake appendicitis. She wondered which side had the appendix and what the symptoms were like.

"I can take that for you," Mrs. Vincent said.

Sophie surrendered the dish mutely, staring in horror as Mrs. Vincent introduced Dylan's mom to Sophie's mom. The two grandmothers . . . in the same room.

"Sophie, I see your chin recovered," Mrs. Morris said.

Sophie reached up to touch her chin.

"From your fall at the lake. Remember?"

"Oh yeah." Sophie just stood there dumbly.

"You go watch the game," Mrs. Vincent said. "We've got plenty of helping hands in here."

"But I could—"

"No, no," Mrs. Morris said. "Go join the kids and the guys. We want to talk about things like menopause and Botox now."

Sophie left the kitchen, but instead of going to the den, she went to Carrie Anne's bedroom and sat down on her bed. What to do, what to do, what to do?

"What are you doing in here?" Carrie Anne asked. "I've been looking all over for you."

Sophie just sat there.

"Are you sick or something?"

She nodded.

"Seriously? What's wrong?"

Sophie didn't respond.

"Want me to get your mom?"

She shook her head.

"Really, Sophie, what's wrong? I mean, you actually do look sick—"

"I think I have mono," Sophie told her. Yes, it was a lie. A big fat lie. But it was all she could come up with at the moment. It wasn't like she could confess to Carrie Anne that (1)she was freaking that Dylan was downstairs, (2) she'd had sex with him, and (3) she was pregnant with his child. Seriously, Carrie Anne would totally freak. Or, worse, she wouldn't believe her.

"Mono?"

Sophie just nodded.

"How'd you get it?"

"Probably from Wes."

Carrie Anne giggled. "You've kissed Wes?"

Sophie started to cry.

"I'm sorry. I'm not making fun of you. But it's just that you never told me." Carrie Anne frowned. "I cannot believe you didn't tell me, Sophie. We're best friends and you keep something like that from me?"

Sophie flopped facedown on the bed and continued to cry.

"What should I do?"

"Nothing," Sophie sobbed. "Just leave me alone."

"Does your mom know you have mono?" Carrie Anne's voice was quieter now. Like she didn't want anyone in her family to hear her.

"No," Sophie muttered.

"Did you go to the doctor?"

"No." Sophie sat up, wiping her cheeks with the backs of her hands.

"So how do you know?"

"Because Wes has it. And I have all the symptoms. Remember how tired I've been?"

"Yeah, I guess. I mean, before, I did. You seem more like your old self lately. Well, except for now."

"Right."

"Why don't you stay up here and have a little rest," Carrie Anne suggested.

"Thanks."

"I need to go back down. I promised Dylan that I'd whoop him in Ping-Pong." Carrie Anne giggled again. "Don't tell Drew, okay?"

"Tell Drew what?" Sophie shook her head. "Huh?"

"You know, I wouldn't want Drew to think I was flirting with Dylan."

"Are you?"

"Duh." Carrie Anne stood up and went to the mirror, where she put on some lip gloss and fluffed her hair. "Wouldn't you?" She held up her hand, examining her delicate gold purity ring. She paused to polish the small diamond on her slim-fitting jeans, checked it again, then smiled and looked at Sophie. "Feel better, okay?"

"Okay."

As Carrie Anne left, Sophie thought about the purity party that Pastor Vincent had hosted when Carrie Anne turned twelve. Naturally all of Carrie Anne's girlfriends were invited, plus their dads. And naturally Sophie's dad declined the invitation. He had to work, he'd said, but Sophie knew that if it had been one of Bart's ball games, Dad would've made the time.

Pastor Vincent had made a sweet speech about Carrie Anne, then he'd presented her with the beautiful ring and they'd danced together. The other fathers, all members of the church, followed suit. Then, as if he felt sorry for Sophie, Pastor Vincent made a little speech and danced with her too. But there was no ring. Not that she'd expected one.

"Sophie?"

Sophie looked up from where she'd been daydreaming to see Mrs. Vincent peering into the bedroom. Why hadn't Carrie Anne shut the door?

"Are you okay?"

"I'm fine." Sophie forced a smile. "Just cramps, you know?"

"Oh, don't I. Did you take some Advil?"

Sophie nodded. "Yeah. I should be fine in a few minutes."

"Good." Mrs. Vincent frowned slightly. "I read your article in the school paper, Sophie."

Sophie braced herself.

"Mrs. North asked me to read it." She made a faint smile. "It was well written . . ."

"But?"

"But . . . I think Mrs. North could be right about the message it sends." She waved her hand. "Oh, not your article so much, Sophie. You're simply reporting what's going on. In fact, we should be thankful that you've brought this issue to the surface. Because it does seem that the school is encouraging promiscuity."

"Encouraging promiscuity?"

"Well, that might be an exaggeration on my part. But for the school to give pregnant girls special attention, special classes, child care . . . well, it does raise some questions."

"I suppose it does."

"And sometimes it's up to us as a church to stand up and be a moral compass to the community. Don't you think?"

Sophie nodded.

"Oh, I could go on and on, but it's about time to check the turkey. I hope you feel well enough to sit down to eat with us, Sophie."

"Me too . . . but I'm not sure."

"Well, you just rest. I'll let your mom know you're under the weather."

"Thanks."

This time Sophie closed the door. Then she curled up on the bed, covering herself with Carrie Anne's thick pink chenille throw. If anyone else came in, she would pretend to be sleeping. She would pretend to sleep the entire day away.

"Hey, wake up, sleepyhead," Carrie Anne said.

"Huh?" Sophie sat up. Apparently she'd fallen asleep for real.

"Mom wants to know if you're coming down for dinner or not."

"Not."

"Man, what is with you people?"

"What?"

"First you're not feeling well. Then Dylan gets sick and leaves—"

"Dylan's gone?" Sophie tried not to look too happy.

"Yeah. Your brother's game had just started, and your dad is pointing Bart out and asking why you aren't there to watch, so I'm making excuses for you, saying that you don't feel so great. And the next thing I know, Dylan has this severe headache and takes off. What a bunch of party poopers."

Sophie patted Carrie Anne's shoulder. "Sorry about that. But the nap actually helped. I feel okay now." Sophie had no doubt that Dylan had left after realizing she was here. Still, that surprised her a little. Was he suddenly having an attack of conscience? Or did he just hate her as much as she hated him?

15

Although no one had actually invited Sophie to attend the church's "town meeting," she went anyway. She decided that, as a journalist, she needed to be there. She sat in the back, with her coat and her mini recorder on, and listened. What she heard didn't surprise her in the least. It was similar to the rhetoric that she'd heard at school from Kelsey, Hannah, and Carrie Anne, only now it was mostly the grown-ups talking. And they made a bigger effort to "Christianize" the words.

"We're not judging those poor pregnant girls," said Mrs. North, Kelsey's mom, in response to Pastor Vincent's challenge to be more like Jesus. "If anything, we feel sorry for them. And we regret that they are being raised in a society where morals, values, and standards keep getting lower and lower."

"That's right," said Mrs. Johnston, Hannah's mom. "As adults and as Christians, we have to take some responsibility for the warped messages our children are getting. Think of what our children watch on TV or movies, or what they see on the Internet. It's no wonder that girls are getting pregnant all over the place. And for the school to provide special treatment, well, it's just like giving teen pregnancy the *Good Housekeeping* stamp of approval."

Of course, everyone laughed at that.

"I couldn't agree more," Mrs. Vincent said. "As Christians, we need to take a stand and let our views be known." She glanced at her husband. "For Carrie Anne's sake as much as all the children in our community."

"And we need to do it in love," he added.

"Of course," Mrs. North said. Then she went right back to her previous diatribe, telling them about a popular TV show with a pregnant teen in the cast. "For all we know, teen pregnancy could be the latest fad. It's time we as parents draw the line."

On and on they went. It seemed everyone wanted to be heard, but there was hardly a dissenter in the group. Well, except for Sophie. Not that she was saying anything. To be fair, it wasn't that she disagreed—in fact, many of the things they were saying were true. It was just that they didn't get it. Not fully. Sophie had seen how the girls needed the pregnancy center. And she couldn't imagine where the girls would be without it.

Finally she couldn't stand it anymore. "May I say something?" she shouted out during a brief pause.

"Of course." Pastor Vincent waved Sophie forward. "It would be great to hear a teen's view."

Sophie could feel the eyes of her friends' parents on her. She suspected they weren't pleased to see that she was here or that she was speaking out. Not that she cared. "Some of you know that I wrote a human interest piece about the pregnancy center for our school paper. Maybe that's why some of you are here." She glanced at Kelsey's mom. "But what you may not know is that I spent time with these girls. They are real girls who are going through a very difficult time, and I just don't—"

"Of course they're going through a difficult time," Mrs. North interrupted. "They are teens and they are pregnant. That can't be easy. But it's a result of bad choices and a lack of—"

"Excuse me, Mrs. North," Pastor Vincent said. "But I believe Sophie was speaking." He turned to Sophie. "Continue, please."

"Okay." She looked evenly at her listeners. "This is my question for all of you. What would you have these girls do? Where would you have them go? Would you lock them away? Would you take away their right to an education? Would you punish them? Tell me, what would you do to replace the pregnancy center?"

"You don't seem to understand our concerns here, Sophie." This came from Carrie Anne's mom. "We acknowledge that you're a good journalist, and we appreciate that you brought this problem to our attention. But you just don't seem to grasp what's at stake here. You don't seem to fully understand."

"What do I *not* seem to fully understand?" Sophie could feel her heart pounding. She knew she was close to losing it.

"Okay." Mrs. Vincent stood. "Let me tell you about Hawaii."

Sophie blinked. "Hawaii?"

"Yes. Did you know that the state of Hawaii has teen pregnancy facilities in most of their public schools?"

Sophie shook her head.

"And did you know that the state of Hawaii has the twelfth highest teen pregnancy rate in the nation?"

She shook her head again.

"So you see, if you build it, they will come."

"Huh?"

"If the school provides a teen pregnancy facility, if they create a comfy, cozy place for pregnant teens to gather, if they choose to accommodate pregnant teens, and if they offer free child care, special classes, counseling, and all those little perks, naturally the girls will think that it's perfectly acceptable to get pregnant. If you build it, they will come."

The room erupted into applause and cheers, and for a moment, Sophie was totally dumbfounded. But she was not ready to back down just yet. "So, are you saying that girls will get pregnant on *purpose*? Or that the girls I interviewed in the pregnancy center *wanted* to get pregnant?"

"I'm saying that the school is sending the message that it's okay. They're making it easy for girls to treat sex casually, to get pregnant, and to have babies. They're making it easy for these girls to have it all. Easy breezy."

"You think those girls have it *easy*?"

"Remember what happened in Gloucester not that long ago," Mrs. North said suddenly. "That high school had a pregnancy center, and the next thing you know they had a regular pregnancy epidemic on their hands."

"That's right," a man in the back shouted. "I heard those girls made a pregnancy pact together. If that's not getting pregnant on purpose, I don't know what is."

"I heard there are thirty girls in Brewster's pregnancy center this year," Mrs. North said. "When it first started, there were less than a dozen."

Sophie wanted to point out those numbers had increased when Brewster decided to include the Maxwell High students as well, but she knew no one would hear her over the din in the room. Everyone was talking at once, spewing out opinions like they were facts.

Sophie glanced over at Pastor Vincent, who seemed a bit overwhelmed too. She made her way back to her seat, gathered her things, and slipped out the back. All she wanted was to run and forget this whole thing. Why had she come? What good had it done?

The next week wasn't starting out much better. Word got out that another kind of town meeting was being held. In city hall. And it would be a media event. Mrs. Manchester had gathered up her cohorts to speak out and had even coerced Sophie into speaking.

"But what will I say?" Sophie had asked her. "Who wants to listen to me?"

"Just say what you said in the paper. Tell them about the girls you met and why you think the pregnancy center is valuable to them."

"I don't know . . ."

"How would you feel, Sophie," she said, staring directly into Sophie's eyes, "if you were in their shoes and no one wanted to stand up and speak for you?"

"Okay." Sophie sighed. "I'll say something."

Mrs. Manchester clasped Sophie's hand. "Bless you."

So when the time came, Sophie got up. She reiterated what she'd written in her article and how the girls she'd met really needed the center. "Think about it," she challenged her listeners. "How will it help those teens if there is no center? How will it help if they don't get an education? How does it help anything when teen mothers don't have enough education to get decent-paying jobs? Do you want them all to end up on welfare? Sure, they made mistakes, but who hasn't? These girls are paying for their mistakes. Why make life harder for them?"

She looked out over the audience with uncertainty. She recognized some faces from church. But she had no idea where the others all stood. Maybe she didn't care. "A long time ago, when a certain woman was thrown in front of Jesus and the people wanted to stone her because she had sinned, Jesus invited the person who had never sinned to throw the first stone. And you know what?" She noticed her pastor's face in the back of the room, and he was nodding like he agreed with her. "No one threw a stone. Maybe that's what we need to do too."

As she left the podium, a lot of people started to clap. She wasn't sure if the ones from her church were clapping too, but she did see Pastor Vincent give her two thumbs up from where he was standing along the back wall. She gave him a grateful nod. Now if only he would embrace that same attitude when he heard the news about her. Not that she planned on telling him—or anyone else for that matter. But eventually . . . well, she knew that some things couldn't be hidden forever.

Just as she returned to her seat to wait for the next speaker, Wes wedged himself onto the bench beside her. "Way to go."

"Thanks." She took in a shaky breath. "That was so freaky."

To her shock he reached over and took her hand. Her hands were still trembling, but she was surprised at how comforting it was to feel the warmth of his hand wrapped around hers. Almost as if he really knew what she was going through, almost as if he understood. And it almost made her cry.

After the meeting, Wes walked her to her car. "What do your parents think of all this?" he asked as they stood in the dimly lit underground parking structure.

"They don't really know."

"They don't know?"

"Well, they're busy."

"Do they read the school paper?"

She shrugged. "I've left issues lying around the house. If they've read it, they haven't mentioned it."

"Do they watch the local news?"

"My mom says the news depresses her, and my dad just watches sports networks."

Wes looked slightly stunned. "Wow. That must be kind of cool."

"Cool?"

"I mean cool as in kind of a relief. My parents are way interested in everything I do. They're the nosiest people on the planet. Believe me, it can be a pain."

"Guess I'm lucky."

Wes made a half smile. "You know, Sophie . . ."

"What?"

"Well, if you ever want to really talk . . . I'm here for you."

She frowned. "Meaning?"

"Meaning . . . sometimes I get the feeling you're carrying this heavy burden."

"Seriously?" She made a contorted face and acted like she was lifting some huge weight.

"Funny." He got serious again. "And sometimes I get the feeling that you use humor as your smoke screen."

"Seems like you've given this a fair amount of thought." She frowned at him. "Guess you take after your parents."

He chuckled. "Okay, now that actually was funny."

"Thank you," she said in her Elvis voice. "Thank you very much."

"But really, Sophie. If you ever need someone to talk to or a shoulder to lean on, I am seriously here for you." He looked directly into her eyes. "I mean that."

She felt a lump growing in her throat as she nodded. "Thanks, Wes. I know you do."

"You're a cool girl." He smiled. "One of the coolest people I know. But even cool people need someone to talk to sometimes."

"Yeah." Her voice sounded husky. She was afraid she was going to cry.

"And even though I'm not as strong a Christian as you are—by the way, that was a great ending to your speech—I am a believer. I'm just not really vocal about it."

"Really?"

He nodded. "Of course, some people don't think Episcopalians are really Christians, but I happen to know that I am."

"That's cool." To her own surprise, she threw her arms around him and hugged him hard. "Thanks, Wes."

"Thank *you*!" He grinned as she stepped away.

Okay, it wasn't like she'd kissed him. And really, she was not ready for that. She didn't know if she'd ever be ready for that again. But it was good to know he was there for her. In her corner. The big question once again was, would he be there for her if he knew? How would a guy feel to know that a girl he really liked was pregnant with another guy's baby?

"Sophie Ramsay," she told herself as she pulled out of the parking structure, "you are a living, breathing soap opera!" As she drove down the street, something caught her eye. She slowed down by First Christian Church and saw that there was a well-lit nativity scene out front. Not one of those cheesy plastic versions but one made of wood, with characters that looked semirealistic and a real wood stable and manger with hay.

She parked her car in front of the church and got out. Since it was a Thursday night, the place was quiet and devoid of onlookers. So she just stood there gazing at the figures and thinking. Sophie knew that Mary had been a pregnant teenager too—and unmarried at that. Of course, it had been God's doing and an incredible honor. Yet Sophie suspected that Mary could relate to her dilemma.

"What should I do, God?" Sophie said aloud. "What?" It was the first time she'd prayed a genuine prayer to God in ages, and she wasn't even sure if he'd want to listen. "I know I messed up," she continued. "I know you must be disappointed in me. And I'm sorry. I'm really sorry. I've told you that about a hundred times. But you haven't told me what I need to do. Tell me what to do."

She waited and waited. Shivering in the chilly December air, she buttoned her jacket up to her chin, turned up the collar, and waited some more. What she was waiting for was unclear. Perhaps a miracle or a bolt of lightning or maybe even a single star as a sign of hope. But nothing happened.

At least nothing out of the ordinary. The truth was, something *was* happening. A calm, quiet voice was whispering inside of her. A voice she knew belonged to God. And as much as she didn't want to hear this particular message—or to even admit that she'd been ignoring it for months now—she knew that God was making himself perfectly clear. God wanted her to confess her sin and to ask for forgiveness, but not only with him this time. That was a good start, but it was not enough. Deep within her she knew what she needed to do, and she wanted to do it. She wanted to obey God.

The only problem was that to obey God meant she would have to tell the truth. She would have to confess to her family and everyone that she had blown it big-time. She would have to admit that she'd broken her purity pledge and that she'd lied to cover it up.

Yet, could admitting the truth be any worse than the lie she was living now? Humiliating, yes. But perhaps it would be a relief.

"Okay, God." She took in a deep breath. "I want to obey you." Once again she confessed—fully and without any reservation— what she'd done. Then she asked God to forgive her. And just like that, she knew he had forgiven her. She also knew that her work here had only begun. She couldn't imagine how difficult it was going to be—certainly the hardest thing she'd ever done in her life. But she knew she had to do it.

"Please help me, God," she prayed. "Help me to be brave and strong. Show me how to do it . . . and where to begin." She took in one last, deep breath of cold night air, said, "Amen," then hurried back to the warmth of her car.

As she drove toward home, she had no idea how she would begin to untangle the web of deceit she had woven, but she believed that with God's help, she could do it. Once she'd truly owned up to her mistake, once she'd laid it at his feet, he'd forgiven her, just like he'd promised. She could feel it inside of her, like the horrible weight of it had been lifted. She knew that God still loved her and that he had fully forgiven her.

Now the big question was, would anyone else?

16

Maybe it was due to the town meeting and the subsequent media coverage. Or maybe it had to do with the Christmas season and a general feeling of goodwill toward men (and pregnant teens) among the community. In any case, not only did the attack against the pregnancy center mostly disintegrate, but people began volunteering to help out with it. Including, Sophie discovered a few days before Christmas break, her best friend's mother.

"What are you doing here, Sophie?" Mrs. Vincent asked as they entered the center simultaneously.

Sophie took in a quick stabilizing breath and waited while Mrs. Vincent signed in on the visitors' list. It had been almost a week since Sophie had made things right with God. Since that night, she had prayed to him many times a day and asked him to lead her on a daily basis. But so far she had confessed nothing to anyone. She had started to a couple of times, like once with Carrie Anne and another time with her mom, but for one reason or another, the timing seemed all wrong. Or maybe Sophie was just a big chicken.

Now, standing there in the pregnancy center with Carrie Anne's mom looking at her with a questioning expression, Sophie felt not only uneasy but also desperate. What if Mrs. Vincent knew somehow? What if she was about to guess the real reason Sophie was there? "Uh, I was about to ask you the same thing, Mrs. Vincent." Sophie took the pen from her. "Why are you here?"

"Carrie Anne may have told you that I used to be an RN."

Sophie just nodded, turning away to sign herself in. Earlier in the week she'd made an appointment with Mrs. Manchester. She'd hoped to have been further along in her confession plan by now. She'd thought that Mrs. Manchester could give her some advice, perhaps even enlist her in the pregnancy program after the holidays—because Sophie doubted that she'd want to show her face in her regular classes by then. But how was she going to spill the beans with her best friend's mother in the next room?

"Before we had kids," Mrs. Vincent continued, "I worked in the maternity ward and taught birthing classes at the hospital, and since I have some spare time, I volunteered to teach the birthing class here next semester. I came today just to look around."

"Really?" Sophie felt the blood rush to her face as she set down the pen. "You'll be teaching here too?"

Mrs. Vincent smiled. "Yes. I thought you might appreciate hearing that. Now tell me, Sophie, what *are* you doing here?"

Despite Sophie's recent resolve to come clean with family and friends and to stop the lies, she couldn't blow her cover just now. Not like this. "I thought I'd do a follow-up story," she said quickly. "For the last newspaper of the year."

"Oh, that's a nice idea."

"Yeah. Kind of a happy Christmas piece. After all the recent controversy, I wanted to write something positive about the center and the girls." Sophie brightened. "And now I can include a bit about how more volunteers are stepping in to help—like you."

"Just for the record, I haven't changed all my views on this issue, but I suppose I've changed my strategy." She reached over and squeezed Sophie's hands. "You were right, Sophie, these girls do need our love and support. Thanks for helping me to see that."

Sophie nodded. But the irony was inescapable. Not long ago, she had faced off with Mrs. Vincent over the teen pregnancy controversy. Now it was likely that, before long, Sophie would be a student in her childbirth class. But she wasn't going to think about that today.

"Sophie," Mrs. Manchester said. "So good to see you again. What can I do for you today?"

With Mrs. Vincent still listening, Sophie quickly retold her most recent fib. "I wanted to write something upbeat and positive for the Christmas edition of the paper," she said. "If I could do another interview with the same girls, it'd be helpful."

"That's a lovely idea." Mrs. Manchester actually hugged Sophie. "So thoughtful of you."

Sophie bit her lip. Why couldn't she just tell the truth? Once and for all she should just spew it out—tell the truth and take the consequences!

"Sophie is always thinking of others," Mrs. Vincent gushed. "Such a fine role model."

Sophie felt like gagging. She hated herself, hated her lies— she was such a pathetic hypocrite! And yet she just stood there accepting this praise like she deserved it.

Mrs. Manchester nodded with enthusiasm. "You *are* a treasure, Sophie. Why don't you go set your interview things up in my office, and I'll go find the girls. By the way, I think Serena has someone she'd like you to meet."

Sophie went to the office and got out her notebook. She hadn't brought the mini recorder, but she could at least take notes and put on the pretense of an interview. Besides, now she had to write that article, hopefully in time to make the final edition of the year. Not only that, but this would give her a chance to talk to Natasha. Her story was so similar to Sophie's that it gave Sophie hope. Natasha, although a year younger, had somehow managed to face up to the truth— somehow she was dealing with it. Maybe Natasha could help—

"Hey, Sophie," Serena said as she entered the office with a chubby-cheeked infant in her arms, "this is my little man, Gilbert."

"Nice to meet you, Gilbert." Sophie grinned down at the baby. Dressed in a red and white Christmas outfit and matching stocking hat, he looked ready to pose for a Christmas card. "Interesting name."

"It was my grandpa's. Now he was a good man."

"So, how is life going for you and Gilbert?"

Serena let out a sigh. "Let me tell you, it is so not easy."

"I'll bet."

"I mean, I thought I was tired before I had my little rug rat. But now it seems like I'm barely keeping one foot in front of the other. He eats all night long. And diaper duty—ew! I think he takes after his daddy in the stinky-pants department."

Sophie chuckled. "Has his daddy seen him?"

"Oh yeah. He came to the hospital and everything."

"So you guys are back together?"

"No way."

"Oh."

"I don't even want him in my life anymore. Well, to see his son. That's okay. But I'm like so over him now. My mama tried to tell me that Reggie was a selfish jerk a long time ago, but I just never listened." She shook her head. "Lots of stuff I never listened about."

"But you're listening now?"

She laughed. "Not according to my mama."

Sophie asked her a few more questions, but it wasn't long before Gilbert was fussing. "He wants to eat again." Serena pushed the pacifier back in his mouth, but he wasn't interested. Soon he was screaming. "And then he's gonna need a change. Are you done?"

"Yeah. Thanks for helping." Sophie watched as Serena juggled the howling baby, shoved the pacifier into the diaper bag, then finally stood. "You and Gilbert have a good Christmas," Sophie told her.

Serena bounced him. "We will," she shouted to be heard over the wailing baby. "You should see all the 'baby's first Christmas' stuff I got for him. He's gonna be the life of the party."

"I'll bet." Sophie actually thought Gilbert could shut down a party.

"Want me to tell Natasha to come?"

Sophie nodded. She was eager to see Natasha. She wanted to hear more about the college boyfriend and his parents. How had Natasha broken the news to them? Who did she tell first? Sophie knew these were self-serving questions and probably had little or nothing to do with a follow-up article, but she wanted to know.

Unfortunately Natasha wasn't feeling chatty. The most Sophie learned was that Natasha initially told her mom, then her mom took over.

"So your mom told Terrence and his family for you?"

"Pretty much." Natasha frowned at Sophie. "But I can't imagine how that's anything you'd print in the newspaper. What's up anyway?"

"Oh, you know . . . just trying to let readers walk a mile in your moccasins."

"Tell them to get pregnant then."

"Yeah, I'm sure that would make an interesting article."

With her hands resting on top of her tummy, Natasha leaned forward. "What's your game, newsgirl?" Her eyes narrowed.

"Huh?"

"Why are you asking me all these questions?"

"For an article on—"

"I don't believe you." Natasha stood. "I think you came here to gawk at us like we're a bunch of sideshow freaks, and it somehow makes you feel better to—"

"That's not it at all."

But it was too late. Natasha was already storming out of the room. Sophie considered chasing after her, apologizing, maybe even explaining. But now Leah was coming in, and she seemed troubled too. Sophie wondered if Natasha had said something to tip her off.

"Are you feeling okay?" Sophie asked as Leah eased herself down into the chair across from Sophie.

Leah sighed. "It's been a rough week."

"How so?" Sophie picked up her pen and notepad, determined to keep this official. Although she was starting to have doubts about her article.

"You're still not going to use my name in the newspaper, right?"

"Right."

Leah had tears in her eyes. "We broke up."

"You and your boyfriend broke up?"

Leah nodded as she pulled out a tissue from the box on Mrs. Manchester's desk.

"I'm so sorry, Leah." Sophie set down her pen.

"Yeah, me too."

"Do you think it might be for the best?"

"I don't know. I mean, I really thought we were getting married, you know, like I told you, right after Christmas. I got a dress and everything."

"That must be hard."

"Yeah . . . last weekend, like straight out of the blue, he told me he's too young to be a dad. He thinks he needs to go to college. Just community college, but he says he needs to go so he can get a better job."

"That sounds smart."

"Smart? To leave me like that?"

"No, I mean smart to get an education."

Leah stared with red-rimmed eyes. "But what about me? What about the baby? What will we do? Why is it okay for me to deal with this on my own?"

Sophie had no answer to that.

"I mean, it takes two to have a baby, right? Shouldn't he have to stick around and help out?"

"I think the father should take some responsibility." Sophie swallowed hard. Words were cheap.

"He promised to marry me." Leah was sobbing again.

Sophie grabbed her a couple more tissues and waited.

"What am I going to do?" Leah said finally.

Like Sophie had answers. "What do you *want* to do?" Sophie knew that Leah was due in late January. Not all that far off.

"I don't know." Leah twisted the tissue into a snake shape. "My parents are pushing me to give it up . . . you know, for adoption."

"How do you feel about that?"

"Confused."

Sophie nodded. "Yeah, I can imagine."

Something in Leah seemed to change just then. Kind of like she snapped from hopelessness to anger. She glared at Sophie. "Really?" she seethed. "You think *you* can imagine? Get real. You're the editor of the school paper. You've probably got a dozen college scholarships all lined up already. I mean, you're free to do whatever you want with your freaking perfect little life. And you want me to believe that *you* can imagine what it's like to be me? Give me a break."

Sophie pressed her lips together and looked down at her nearly blank notepad. So much for the Christmas story. There was a long silence, finally broken by the loud blowing of Leah's nose.

"Sorry," Leah muttered. "I didn't mean to lose it."

"It's okay." Sophie closed her notebook.

"So . . . are we done now? I mean, I think I've said way more than enough."

"Yeah, we're done. Thanks." They both stood, then Sophie reached out and put a hand on Leah's arm. "Things aren't always what they seem, Leah."

Leah looked slightly confused, but she nodded like she got it.

"I'll see you after Christmas, okay?"

"Yeah, sure." There was a strong note of cynicism in Leah's voice as she turned to leave.

Sophie held on to Leah's arm. "Wait a minute."

"Huh?" Leah looked startled. "What's wrong?"

"I *will* see you after Christmas, Leah."

"Yeah, sure . . . whatever."

"I mean I'll see you here—here in the pregnancy center."

"Another article?"

"No." Sophie's heart was pounding. "I'll be *coming* here."

"Oh, let me guess. You're going to do one of those assignments where the reporter comes in and pretends to be one of us for a day or two?" Leah rolled her eyes. "Wear one of those pregnancy packs?"

"No, Leah. I mean I'll be here *as* one of you." Sophie couldn't believe she was about to say it. "I'm pregnant."

Leah looked skeptical. "Yeah, right."

"I really am." Sophie pulled up her baggy shirt, exposing her rounded tummy.

"Oh." Leah's eyes grew wide.

195

"I'm not even a full five months yet, but I'm showing."

"Yeah." Leah nodded. "You are."

"And you're the first person I've told."

She blinked. "Really?"

Sophie pulled her shirt back down. "Really. So I'd appreciate it if you'd keep it quiet for now."

"I understand."

"I planned to tell my family this week . . . but it's been hard finding the right moment."

"Good luck with that." Leah shook her head in a dismal way.

"Yeah, thanks."

Suddenly Leah reached out and hugged Sophie. "It'll be okay. You'll get through it. Somehow we'll all get through it. Right?"

Sophie had tears in her own eyes now. "I hope so."

17

Sophie had been praying for an opportune moment to break the news to her parents. When her mom came home from work early, it seemed the time had come.

"I need to talk to you." Sophie was sitting at the kitchen table, watching her mom put away a few groceries.

"Sure, hon." Mom closed the fridge door, then reached for a box of Raisin Bran.

"Uh, you might want to sit down."

Mom turned and looked at Sophie. "Something wrong?"

Sophie felt the blood draining from her face as she nodded.

Mom set the cereal on the counter and came over to the table. "What is it? Something bad happen at school? You didn't wreck the car, did you?" She shook her head. "No, I saw it on the street. It was—"

"Mom." Sophie wanted to break the rambling flow of her mom's words.

"What is it?"

"I'm pregnant."

Mom's jaw dropped. *"What?"*

"I said, I'm pregnant."

"Are you just jerking my chain, Sophie, because if you are, this isn't even a tiny bit funny."

"I'm totally serious."

Mom reached for a kitchen stool, slowly lowering herself onto it with her eyes locked onto Sophie. "You're pregnant?"

Sophie just nodded, waiting for the full realization of this to sink in.

"You're *really* pregnant?" Mom shook her head in disbelief. "How is that even possible?"

Sophie frowned. "I think you know all about the birds and the bees by now, Mom."

"No, I mean, *how is that possible?*" Mom's voice was louder now. "Sophie, you don't even have a boyfriend. How can you possibly be pregnant?"

"If discussing and analyzing this could change the outcome, I'd be all for it. But the hard fact is that I *am* pregnant."

"What about your purity pledge?"

"Unfortunately it's not an inoculation against pregnancy."

"But you took it so seriously."

"Apparently not seriously enough."

"This just seems impossible, Sophie. How do you even know for sure that you're really pregnant?"

"I've taken some pregnancy tests."

Mom's face paled. "And?"

"And they were positive." Sophie felt irritated. Why was Mom being so dense about this? Did she think it made this any easier?

"But maybe they were wrong."

"No, I have all the symptoms too."

"But it could be something—"

"Mom!" Sophie shouted. "I *am* pregnant. Okay?"

"No, Sophie. It is not okay. It is not okay for you to be pregnant, do you understand?"

"What are you saying?"

"Why?" Tears ran down Mom's face. "Why did you go and ruin your life like this? Why? You're not that kind of girl, Sophie. You've never been that kind of girl. Why did you do this?"

"I didn't do it on purpose."

"Who?" Mom demanded. "Who is the father?"

"Does it matter?"

"Of course it matters. The father is 50 percent responsible too."

"That's a statistic, Mom, not a reality."

"I don't know how you let this happen, Sophie. What were you thinking?"

"Obviously I wasn't thinking."

"But you're too smart to do this. Too smart to ruin your life like this."

"Intelligence has nothing to do with fertility."

"But I didn't even know you were sexually active."

"Did you think I was going to tell you?"

Mom fished a rumpled tissue from her sweater pocket and wiped her tears. "I just don't understand. I do not understand. You had a purity pledge. I thought you were such a good girl."

"Mom." Sophie's voice softened. "I'm really, really sorry." She was crying now too. "I hate that I've done this to you. And to Dad."

"Dad!" Mom looked at the clock. "What are we going to do about your dad, Sophie?"

"Besides tell him?"

"He's going to have a cow."

"I know."

"Are you absolutely, 100 percent sure that you're really pregnant?"

"I'm not making it up."

"When was your last period?"

"Early August."

Mom looked totally stunned. "Early August?"

Sophie just nodded.

"How long have you *known* you were pregnant?"

"Since early September."

"And you never told me?" Mom looked truly hurt.

"I never told anyone."

"So you're"—Mom counted on her fingers—"five months along?"

"Not quite."

"Oh, Sophie."

"I really am sorry, Mom. I know how disappointed you must be. I know I've hurt you. I hope you'll be able to forgive—"

"Honey, I'm home," her dad's voice boomed. Then he was in the kitchen. Before he peeled off his jacket, his cheerful demeanor vanished. "What's wrong?" he demanded.

They said nothing, just sat there.

"Bart?" he exclaimed. "Something's happened to Bart?"

"No." Mom shook her head. "Something's happened to Sophie."

He looked confused. "But she's sitting right here. What's happened?"

"Dad." Sophie took a deep breath. "I'm really, really sorry to tell you this. I hope you'll be able to forgive me—"

"What?" His eyes widened with fear. "What did you do? Trouble at school? With the law?"

"I wish." Sophie glanced at Mom for support.

"Just plain trouble," Mom muttered.

"What?" Dad looked irritated. "Will someone please tell me what the heck is going on here?"

"I'm pregnant, Dad."

His face froze, and he pulled out a chair and sank down into it.

"I'm really sorry to disappoint—"

"You can't be pregnant!"

"She is, Bud."

"But she made that whole abstinence pledge." He wouldn't even look at her. He pounded his fist on the table. "This is that stupid church's fault. They set girls up to think they're better than everyone else, and then they fall down just the same—"

"The church had nothing to do with it," Mom said.

"Says you!"

Suddenly her parents were fighting about it, acting as if she wasn't even in the room. Dad blamed Mom for not having taken Sophie in for some kind of birth control. Mom blamed Dad for not having been involved in the purity party that Pastor Vincent had put together. As they screamed and yelled, Sophie slipped out of the kitchen and up to her room. She wished she were dead.

As the yelling continued, Sophie curled up on her bed, pulled her pillow over her head to muffle the noise, and eventually fell asleep. When she woke up, it was to the sound of her mother's calm voice.

"Are you okay, sweetie?"

Sophie sat up and looked at Mom. "Huh?"

"Sorry about that little fireworks show downstairs."

"Is Dad okay?"

Mom frowned. "Let's just say he's gone out to think about it."

"To a bar, you mean?"

Mom shrugged and sat down on Sophie's bed. "I'm so sorry," she said. "I feel like this is partially my fault."

"Why?" Sophie said. "Because Dad made you feel guilty?"

"Because I do feel guilty."

"Why should you feel guilty? I'm the one who blew it."

"I should've talked to you more. I should've suspected that something was wrong. I know you've been acting differently. But I just figured it was another adolescent thing."

"Yeah, a pregnant adolescent thing."

"I assume you decided against an abortion." Mom looked away as she said this. "I mean, I know about your religious beliefs, and I respect that."

"I actually went to a family planning clinic to get an abortion."

"Oh, Sophie. And you didn't even tell me?"

"I didn't want anyone to know, Mom. I was too ashamed. I still am."

"But you decided not to get an abortion."

"I guess I figured two wrongs couldn't make a right."

"Right." Mom sighed loudly.

"Do you wish I'd gotten an abortion?"

"I don't know . . . I wish you weren't pregnant, Sophie. For your own sake."

"Me too."

"So what do you plan to do—I mean, when the baby comes?"

"I don't know."

Mom just nodded like this wasn't surprising.

"What do you think I should do?"

"Only you know the answer to that, Sophie."

"I mean, I will finish school. No doubt about that. I plan to enroll in the pregnancy center at school."

"Was that why you got so involved in that debate?" Mom said.

"I didn't know that you knew about—"

"I don't live under a rock, Sophie. I knew. I just didn't want to get involved." She pushed her fingertips against her temples.

"I'm really sorry, Mom."

"I know you are, sweetie." Mom put her arms around Sophie. "So am I."

"Do you forgive me?"

"Of course." Mom continued to hug her, stroking her hair. "I love you, Sophie. How could I not forgive you?"

"That might not be the case with Dad."

"He'll get over it . . . in time."

"He wouldn't even look at me."

"I know." She sighed.

"I only had sex twice, Mom." For some reason Sophie wanted to make this perfectly clear. "And I didn't even like it."

"Then why did you do it?"

"The guy . . . I thought—I thought I was in love . . . I thought he loved me." Sophie told her mom all about camp and Dylan and how he'd pulled her in. "It was almost like I was under his spell. I mean, he'd just touch me and say sweet things, and I—I was such a fool." Sophie was crying again. But her mom continued to hold her, rocking her to and fro as Sophie just sobbed and sobbed.

Finally she quit crying, and she and Mom just sat there looking at each other. "What now?" Sophie asked.

"Dinner." Mom stood up. "You need to eat properly when you're pregnant."

"I've been taking prenatal vitamins," Sophie admitted. "I kept them well hidden in my sock drawer."

"Have you been to an obstetrician yet?"

"Not yet."

"Want me to schedule you an appointment with mine? My ob-gyn doctor is nice."

"Yeah, thanks."

Sophie and Mom moved quietly through the remainder of the evening. As if on autopilot, they fixed dinner, then sat down to eat. Sophie did not expect to see her dad again that night. She just prayed that he'd get over it . . . eventually.

"You know . . . you're going to have to tell your brother," Mom said as they cleaned up the dinner things.

"No." Sophie put the remainder of green salad in the fridge.

"You need to do that. Bart deserves to know what's going on."

"In time."

"There's no time like the present." Mom picked up the receiver and handed it to Sophie.

Sophie sighed. "I just don't think I can do it."

"Want me to break it to him for you?"

Sophie felt a rush of relief. "Would you? I mean, I'll talk to him later . . . after he recovers from the shock."

As Mom started to dial his number, Sophie made a quick getaway. She didn't even want to hear her mother's end of that conversation. Instead, she went to her room and began constructing an email to send to him, explaining how it had happened and how horrible she had felt for breaking her promise to God, but that she knew God had forgiven her. She just hoped her brother would too. Then she hit send.

She could still hear Mom downstairs talking to Bart. Sophie didn't think that Bart would call her, but just in case, she turned her cell phone off. She couldn't take any more family emotion tonight.

The next morning, Sophie noticed that Carrie Anne was standing out in the school parking lot, looking around as if she was waiting for someone. Sophie parked her car, then got out and walked over.

"There you are!" Carrie Anne exclaimed. "I've been trying to call your cell phone since last night."

"It was off."

"Sophie!" Carrie Anne's eyes were wide with concern. "Tell me it's not true."

"What's not true?"

"My mom said you were at the pregnancy center yesterday."

"That's true. I was." Sophie braced herself. It was time to tell her best friend. "And I have something—"

"My mom said you're pregnant, Sophie! But I told her no way—if you were pregnant, you would've told me." Carrie

Anne laughed. "I also told her that in order to be pregnant, you'd have to have had sex. And since I know that hasn't happened, I know—"

"Why did your mom say I was pregnant?"

"Some girl there told everyone you were."

"Leah!"

"Yeah, whatever. The point is, we need to do some damage control, Sophie. You don't want the whole school thinking you're pregnant."

"I *am* pregnant."

Carrie Anne just stared at her. "What?"

"I'm pregnant, Carrie Anne. I'm going to have a baby."

"No . . . no way."

"It's true."

Carrie Anne looked like she was going to either faint or be sick. "Sophie?"

"I'm sorry. But it is true."

"No." Carrie Anne firmly shook her head. "You're pulling my leg. I *know* you cannot be pregnant. You're a virgin. Like me."

"I was. But I'm not now."

"Sophie?" Her voice was shrill. "What are you saying?"

"That I was an idiot. That I had sex. Only twice. And it wasn't fun. Then I got pregnant."

"But Sophie . . ." Carrie Anne grabbed both of Sophie's arms and shook her. "That's not possible. You made a pledge."

"I broke it."

"I don't believe you."

"Do you want to see my stomach?"

Carrie Anne glanced around nervously. "No!"

"Look, Carrie Anne, I understand your shock . . . and your disappointment. This hasn't exactly been a walk in the park for me either."

"You really are pregnant?" Her voice sounded small and scared. "My best friend is going to have a baby?"

"Yes, and don't worry, it's not catching."

"Does Wes know?"

Sophie pressed her lips together. "Not yet."

"How do you think he'll handle it?"

"I have no idea."

"So my mom was right after all." Carrie Anne sighed.

"We're late for class," Sophie pointed out.

"Yeah." Carrie Anne started walking toward school. Then she turned to look at Sophie. "In fact, I better make a run for it. I've been late once already this week." She took off.

Sophie watched her best friend running away from her, and somehow she knew that was an image of things to come.

18

The last couple of days before Christmas break were like a walking nightmare for Sophie. Thanks to Leah's big mouth, the whole school seemed to know. Some kids acted like it was no big deal. Some just tossed her the look—she decided it was a weird mixture of sympathy and scorn. Others used the opportunity to make fun of her, saying she must've "caught something" at the pregnancy center.

Naturally Kelsey, Hannah, and even Jenny were all shocked and disappointed, but they at least spoke to her, albeit with judgment. Meanwhile Carrie Anne avoided her like the plague. Yet Sophie was glad the news was out. It felt better to be criticized for something real than to be praised for something false. She was done being a hypocrite.

Still, it wasn't easy. And perhaps the hardest part of what went on at school was how everyone assumed that Wes was the father.

"I'm so sorry they're blaming you," Sophie told him on the second day of her new life as a publicly pregnant girl. They'd met at Starbucks after school to talk. "I've denied it over and over, but you probably seem like the likeliest candidate, and people love to jump to conclusions."

Wes looked truly sad as they sat down with their coffees. It was the first time they'd really spoken since she'd broken the news to him yesterday. But even now he wasn't saying much.

"I guess it's natural that they'd assume it was you," she continued, "since you're the only guy I've ever been seen with."

"Who *is* the father, Sophie?"

"Do you really want to know?"

He nodded, so she told him the whole humiliating story. Well, not everything, since he was a guy, after all. "I just can't believe how lame and gullible I was, Wes. A pathetic fool."

"You know what's really pathetic," he said quietly.

"What?"

"I actually wish I *was* the father."

"Oh, Wes, no, you don't. It's a horrible position to be in when you're a teenager. I wouldn't wish it on anyone—especially not someone I care about."

"What about this Dylan dude? Is he taking any responsibility for, uh, things?"

"He doesn't know yet. I mean, if you hadn't noticed, I've pretty much kept this thing secret."

"The cat's out of the bag now."

"Yeah." She sighed. "Mr. Young still hasn't talked to me about it, but I know he knows. As soon as we're back from Christmas break, I'll resign as editor. And from yearbook too."

"Why?"

"Why?" She looked at him incredulously. "No one will want me doing those things now."

"I would."

"That's because you're kind and forgiving. But seriously, I need to step down. And you'll make a great chief editor, Wes."

"I think you're jumping to some conclusions."

"I think I'm being realistic. Everyone knows now. And I'll be showing soon. The best thing is to just start doing the teen pregnancy center classes. To lie low and wait for D-day."

"Huh?"

"Delivery day."

"Oh yeah, right. And what then?"

"I'm 99 percent sure I'll give the baby up for adoption."

"But that leaves 1 percent unsure."

"I know. And it's a big 1 percent."

"I think you're the bravest girl I know, Sophie."

"Brave or stupid?"

"Brave." He set down his coffee cup. "I can't believe you kept this whole thing secret for so long. Most girls would've fallen totally apart."

"Oh, trust me, I fell apart. Over and over. Just when no one was looking."

"So, how's Carrie Anne with it now? And your other friends?"

"Carrie Anne has been avoiding me like she thinks what I have is seriously contagious. And now I think she's turned

Kelsey against me as well. Hannah has been kind but distant. And Jenny, well, after she laid into me for being ignorant, she's been okay."

"Christians can be so hard on each other."

"They sometimes forget that whole forgiveness thing."

"Which is so weird when you consider that's why Jesus came to earth and everything—to show real forgiveness."

"You know what really worries me," she admitted as they were leaving Starbucks.

"What?"

"Carrie Anne's dad is the pastor of our church, and . . . well, I just can't bear to see the disappointment in his eyes. I mean, he watched me make my purity vow, he danced with me at the party. I know it seems silly since he's not even my father—who still isn't speaking to me, by the way—but I care what he thinks."

"Well, if he's a good pastor, he'll handle it right and forgive you."

Sophie nodded, but based on the behavior of Pastor Vincent's daughter, she had her doubts.

Wes walked her to her car and then hugged her. "I'm here for you, Sophie."

"Thanks. You have no idea how much that means to me right now."

He frowned. "Well, I'm mostly here for you. I forgot that my family is going back east to visit my grandparents for the holidays."

"Oh well. That's okay." She unlocked her car. "I'm just relieved to have Christmas break right now. I so need a vacation from all this."

"Have a merry Christmas, Sophie." He leaned over and kissed her on the forehead.

"Thanks, Wes. Thanks for everything."

As Sophie drove through town, she knew she was going to pass the church. Suddenly she knew what she had to do—she had to face the lion in his den. Okay, Pastor Vincent wasn't a lion. That was more like her own dad. But just the same, she knew it wouldn't be easy. And as she walked through the front foyer, she suddenly questioned her reasoning and was about to make a run for it.

"Sophie Ramsay?" a woman's voice said. Sophie looked to see Mrs. Leopold coming around the corner. She was the church receptionist and the one person at the church who usually knew everything about everyone.

"Hey," Sophie said softly. "Is Pastor Vincent around?"

"I believe he's in his office. Did you have an appointment?"

Sophie shook her head. "No, I just wanted a few minutes with him, but if he's busy I can—"

"No, no, let me just buzz him." She was already on the phone, telling him that Sophie was here, and the next thing Sophie knew, she was being welcomed into his office.

"Have a seat."

"Thanks." She sat down and took a deep breath. "I know you've probably heard by now."

He nodded, folding his hands on his desk.

"But I decided to come speak to you face-to-face."

"I respect that, Sophie."

"I know you're not my father, but you're kind of like a spiritual father, so I know that I've hurt you too. So I just want to say how sorry I am and that I hope you'll forgive me."

His smile seemed genuine. "I already did forgive you."

"You did?"

He nodded. "Trying to set a good example."

"For Carrie Anne?"

"I'm sorry she's being so hard on you, Sophie. If it's any comfort, I think she'll come around."

"I'm not really surprised that she's mad. I mean, I was pretty mad at myself at first. And a lot of times I still am. I can't believe how stupid I was."

"You need to forgive yourself too, Sophie."

"I guess I'll have to work on that."

"So, how are your parents handling it?"

"My mom's actually being really understanding—I mean, once she recovered from the shock. My dad . . . well, he's still angry."

"I'm sorry."

"So am I. Really, really sorry." She shook her head. "If I could turn back the clock, I would. I prayed and prayed at first for God to somehow change things, take the pregnancy away—anything to escape." She pressed her lips together. "I even considered an abortion."

"That's not surprising."

"I was surprised. I mean, you know me, I picketed the abortion clinic. I am totally pro-life. And yet when it impacted my life . . . I wasn't so sure."

He cleared his throat. "Sophie . . . may I ask you something?"

She shrugged. "Why not? My life's pretty much an open book these days."

"Well, Carrie Anne said that you're telling everyone that your boyfriend is not the father of your baby. Is that correct?"

"Yes. Wes is absolutely not the dad. I'd swear it on a stack of Bibles. We've never had sex."

"Carrie Anne said you told her that it was a guy at church camp, is that right?"

She nodded, and now her mouth felt drier than sandpaper. She felt the blood rush to her cheeks, and her pulse rate increased. She hadn't even considered Pastor Vincent's connection to Dylan when she'd come here today. She'd simply wanted to make things right with her pastor.

"Sophie, may I ask who the real father is?"

She swallowed hard. "Can I tell you this in confidence?"

"Certainly."

She took in a deep breath and held it. "Dylan Morris."

Pastor Vincent's blue eyes grew wide. "Dylan Morris?"

She nodded and looked down at her lap. The room was silent. She imagined she could hear Pastor Vincent breathing . . . and her own heart pounding in her ears. Had she really just told him that his best friend's son was responsible for her pregnancy?

"I must say, you've caught me by surprise, Sophie."

She looked up. "You don't believe me?"

"No, I'm not saying that. It's just that—"

"I know. Dylan is a family friend, and he's a good Christian and—"

"Good Christian men make mistakes too, Sophie."

"Yes . . . believe me, I know."

His countenance softened. "Dylan does have a way with the girls." Suddenly Pastor Vincent looked concerned. "Does Carrie Anne know yet?"

"No. I can't even imagine how she'd react if she did."

"She still has quite a crush on Dylan."

"I know."

"This really is a pickle, isn't it?"

Despite herself, Sophie smiled. "Yes, it's a real pickle."

"Does Dylan know about this yet?"

She shook her head. "I—I don't really know how to tell him, Pastor Vincent. I mean, what do I do—just call him up and say, 'Hey, you're gonna be a daddy'?"

"That is rough."

She just nodded.

"Would it help if I got involved?" He paused. "Because you must understand that legally—and for many other reasons—Dylan needs to be informed."

"Would you do that?"

"Under one condition."

"What?"

"You're absolutely certain that Dylan is the father."

Sophie pushed away her feelings of indignation. After all, why shouldn't he ask? This news was shocking—what else might he not know about her? So she told him the whole story—sparing some details—about how they only had sex twice. "The truth is, I wasn't even sure what happened the first time, and I actually told him no. Then the second time, I wanted him to stop . . . but I also wanted him to love me. He said he loved me." She was crying again. Would there come a time when she could tell this story without tears?

Pastor Vincent was taking notes. Did he think this was going to turn into some kind of court case? Or did he plan to use this against her? After all, he was Dylan's friend as much as hers.

He looked up with sad eyes. "I'm so sorry, Sophie."

She blinked. "You're sorry?"

"This should never have happened to you. And at one of our camps." He shook his head. "It's actually making me quite angry."

"I'm sorry, Pastor Vincent. I didn't mean—"

"No, I mean I'm angry at Dylan. I expected more from him. And I suspect that you never would've broken your purity pledge if he hadn't pressured you and taken advantage of you like that. I'm really disappointed in him."

"Now I feel like a tattletale," she admitted.

"The story needs to be told, Sophie. In some ways, it should be shouted from the rooftops."

"You mean *everyone* will know?"

"Maybe everyone needs to know. It's an old story, Sophie—selfish young men taking advantage of innocent young girls, making promises just to get what they want." He actually slammed his fist on the desk. "But when it's a young man who professes to be strong in his faith, well, it just really infuriates me."

"But it's not like I really want to punish Dylan. In some ways, I'd like to just keep the whole thing a secret."

"But what about the child?"

Her hand slipped down to her stomach. "The child?"

"He or she may need to know who both parents are."

"I suppose."

Pastor Vincent's anger was replaced with sadness as he and Sophie wrapped up their discussion. She knew he was hurting for both her and Dylan, and maybe even for Dylan's parents. Surely they would be disappointed too.

She was about to leave, then thought of something. "You're not going to tell Carrie Anne, are you?"

"No. I'll leave that to you."

"To me?"

"Wouldn't it be kinder for her to hear it from you before she hears it from someone else?"

"Maybe." But the truth was, Sophie wasn't too sure. If anything was going to put the final nail into the coffin of what used to be their friendship, this would surely be it.

19

"You cannot be serious." Carrie Anne stared at Sophie like she was seeing a three-headed space alien that had just threatened her life.

"I am serious."

"You expect me to believe that you had sex with Dylan Morris?"

"It's your choice to believe it or not. But it's the truth."

"I think you've lost your mind, Sophie."

"Thanks. There were many times in the last few months when I would've agreed with you."

"You're saying that you and Dylan did it at camp?"

"That's what happened, Carrie Anne." Sophie's voice was flat. "I'm not proud of it."

"And you never told me?"

"I never told anyone. Do you know how ashamed I was? Do you know how humiliating this is? I mean, it was bad enough to know that I'd broken my vow. To realize that Dylan had just used me—"

"Now you're saying he used you?"

Sophie wished she'd done this by phone, and then she could just hang up. But she'd come to Carrie Anne's house and now she was stuck in her bedroom. Maybe she should just leave.

"Dylan isn't like that." Carrie Anne stood in front of her mirror with her hands on her hips.

"Like I said, you can believe what you want to believe, Carrie Anne, but the truth is the truth. And since you obviously have no interest in knowing what the truth is, I think I'll go." Sophie reached for the doorknob.

"Wait." Carrie Anne turned and looked at Sophie with narrowed eyes. "What was Dylan's reaction when you accused him—"

"I haven't accused him of anything. If it wasn't for your dad, Dylan would remain totally out—"

"My dad? What does he have to do with this?"

"He's also my pastor, Carrie Anne. And he offered to speak with Dylan."

Carrie Anne just stood there. Maybe she was speechless.

"Look, I am really, really sorry for how this is hurting you. I would do anything to make it all go away. But life isn't like that. Sometimes your bad choices and mistakes follow you to the grave. That will be the case with this one."

"So what are you going to do?" Carrie Anne's voice softened ever so slightly. "I mean, with the baby?"

"Probably give it up for adoption."

"What if Dylan—if he really is the father, which I'm still not sure about—what if he wanted to do the honorable thing and marry you, Sophie?"

"Are you insane?" Sophie couldn't believe Carrie Anne had just said that. "I don't love him. And he sure doesn't love me. What kind of horrible marriage would that be?"

Carrie Anne frowned. "Not so good. But it might be the right thing to do—you know, for the sake of the baby."

"I think it would be absolutely nuts!" Sophie shook her head. What was wrong with Carrie Anne? "It would be totally and certifiably nuts! And I can promise you that if Dylan ever asked me to marry him, I would most definitely turn him down. I do not love him, and I don't have the slightest shred of respect for him anymore. I can't believe you'd even suggest such stupidity."

"Sorry." Carrie Anne looked hurt.

"No, *I'm* sorry." Sophie sighed. "I feel like all I do is bring people pain. I will understand completely if you don't want to be my friend anymore."

Carrie Anne didn't say anything.

"I just hope that in time you'll forgive me."

Sophie left. She couldn't stand another minute of Carrie Anne's judgment. On one hand, she didn't blame her. How would Sophie have felt if the tables were turned? What if Carrie Anne had broken her pledge and was trekking around school with a big pregnant belly, expecting Sophie to act like nothing had changed, like it was no big deal? Well, it was a big deal, and Sophie knew it. And she didn't blame Carrie Anne or Kelsey or Hannah or Jenny or Wes or anyone for steering clear of her. On the other hand, it hurt to lose a best friend.

Thankfully she would still have the pregnancy center. At least she'd be understood there. She would make friends there too. And she would finish her school year. All thanks to the pregnancy center. She couldn't help but laugh at the irony as she got into her car and drove home. Who would've thought—just a year or even six months ago—that Sophie Ramsay would ever have been thankful for the high school's teen pregnancy center?

❁

Mom, true to her word, made a doctor's appointment for Sophie. While other teenage girls were hanging with friends at the mall, doing some last-minute Christmas shopping and grabbing a movie, Sophie's feet were above her head as the doctor did her "internal exam."

It was the first time Sophie had experienced a gynecological visit, and unfortunately she knew it would not be the last. The worst part was the way the pain down there reminded her of how this baby had been conceived. In pain. Really, why did everyone act like sex was so great? For Sophie it hadn't merely been physically painful, it had annihilated her life.

"Everything looks good." Dr. Phillips removed her latex gloves, tossing them into the metal trash can. "You can sit up now."

Sophie blinked back tears as she removed her feet from the stirrups and sat up, pulling the lap cloth closer to her.

"I'd say that you're just starting your nineteenth week."

Sophie already knew from her research that the average pregnancy lasted forty weeks. "So almost halfway done."

"You got that right. Midway. Some women say this is the most pleasant part of pregnancy."

"Pleasant is not the word I'd use to describe any of this."

The doctor smiled. "Any questions?"

Sophie twisted her mouth to one side. "Kind of."

"Go for it."

"Okay, I only had sex twice," she said quietly. "It hurt a lot the first time. And the second time wasn't much better."

"Seems like a bum deal now, doesn't it?"

Sophie rolled her eyes. "Tell me about it. But anyway, I'm just curious, if sex hurts that much, why is it so popular?"

The doctor laughed. "It usually hurts at the beginning. That's normal. But eventually people figure out how things work. Otherwise I'd be out of business."

Sophie knew her face was red, but at least she'd gotten a straight answer. Not that she ever planned to have sex again.

"So, unless you have more questions, you can go ahead and get dressed, and the nurse will come draw some blood. And don't forget to make another appointment on your way out. Merry Christmas!"

Sophie told the doctor "Merry Christmas" too, but all she could think was that this Christmas was going to be anything but merry at her house. Dad still wasn't speaking to her. Although he'd quit hanging at his favorite bar, he now parked himself in front of the TV with several beers nearby. And he and Mom fought with regularity. Sophie knew it was all thanks to her. Mom said not to worry about it and that Dad was just being immature and selfish. But Sophie knew that it was only because she had been immature and selfish. That hurt.

The other thing that hurt was that Bart hadn't responded to her email. And he hadn't called her. Mom said it was because he was so busy with football and that he was distracted with playoffs. But Sophie thought she knew better.

As relieved as she was to be out of school—away from her "friends"—she couldn't believe how each day, each hour, and each minute seemed to drag on. It felt as if God had reached down and turned time onto slow speed. Consequently she slept a lot. When she wasn't sleeping, she was on pins and needles. She could only assume that Pastor Vincent had spoken to Dylan by now. Possibly his parents as well. What if Dylan called her? Or, worse, what if he came over to her house? Would she even answer the door? She really didn't want to see him. Not alone. Really, not at all. It was easier to just pretend he had nothing to do with this. He was not part of the equation. Less significant than a sperm donor. An unwanted sperm donor.

As it turned out, Christmas wasn't too terrible, although it was definitely strange. Sophie was relieved when the "festivities" were over and Bart headed back to school for his final playoff game. They'd had a brief conversation, and Bart admitted that he was disappointed in her but that he'd forgiven her. Still, she could tell things had changed between them. Like Dad, he was uncomfortable being around her. But at least Dad had started talking to her again. That was something. Not more than a few words at a time, and he continued to avoid her eyes as if he was not only uncomfortable but ashamed of her too. Why shouldn't he be? Why shouldn't everyone be ashamed of her?

Sophie knew she was depressed. But she tried not to show it when her family was around. She knew it was unfair to drag them down with her. So she did all she could to keep things light. She made jokes at her own expense and helped her mom with everything she could think of, but like everything else since her pregnancy, she just wanted the holidays to be over with. And if she could speed up the clock and the calendar, she would. Oh, she had no illusions that she'd ever have a normal life again, but the sooner this stage of her life passed, the happier she'd be. Although being "happy" seemed a bit of a stretch.

The highlight of the holidays was when Wes called on Christmas day. "How's it going?" he asked with so much sympathy that she felt like crying.

"Well, imagine *The Simpsons* if Lisa got pregnant. That might just about describe it."

He laughed. "At least you still have your sense of humor."

"I try."

"I miss you."

"Really?"

"Really. I wish I were with you right now. I'd give you a big hug and tell you that everything's going to be okay."

"I could use that."

"Then consider yourself hugged."

"Thanks."

"I just want you to know that when we're back in school, I am totally there for you. If people want to think I'm the father of your baby, I'm cool with that."

"Seriously?"

"Yeah. And I plan to lobby for you to remain chief editor, Sophie. Unless you really don't want me to."

"I don't really know what I want."

"Well, I've been thinking about it. A lot. I think you have as much right to continue in that role as I would have to take it. I mean, for all everyone knows, I am the father of the baby. Why should you lose everything while the dad gets the 'get out of jail free' card?"

She groaned.

"Have you heard from him? From Dylan?"

Sophie told him about her talk with Carrie Anne's dad. "So my guess is he knows by now."

"What do you think he'll do?"

"Hopefully nothing."

"If he's the jerk I think he is."

"Thanks." She smiled, then told him about Carrie Anne's reaction. Well, everything but her lame suggestion that Sophie and Dylan should get married. And that was out of respect for her ex–best friend because no one should be that clueless.

Wes turned the subject to lighter things, and they talked for about an hour. When she finally hung up, she realized she actually felt better.

On the Saturday morning after Christmas, Pastor Vincent called Sophie's cell phone. Her heart pounded as she answered. After a brief greeting, he got right to it. "Dylan and his parents want to meet with you and your parents, Sophie."

"All of us?" Her voice was tight and high-pitched. "In the same room?"

"I know it won't be easy, Sophie, but it might be necessary."

"My dad . . . I mean, he's kind of unpredictable. What if he says something terrible to them?"

"I'd be surprised if he didn't."

"Really?"

"I'd do the same thing myself if Carrie Anne was in your position. I'd probably knock Dylan's block off . . . in love, of course." He chuckled.

She found this surprisingly comforting. "Thanks."

"You're welcome. Just so you know, I didn't spare his feelings when I confronted him."

"He didn't deny it?" It had occurred to her that he might take that escape route.

"To be honest, he did."

Her heart sank. "Really?"

"Until I reminded him that a simple DNA test could prove him a liar. And then I told him that, as a Christian, he had a responsibility to own up to his mistake. His dad backed me on that."

"And his mom?"

"Naturally she's upset and disappointed . . . and hurt."

"I can imagine." Sophie wanted to add that, although it wasn't easy, it couldn't be nearly as tough as it was for the family of the pregnant girl. Dylan didn't have to go around wearing his bulging belly as a badge of dishonor. He could return to his school, slip under the radar, and pretend that nothing had changed.

Sometimes it was hard not to be bitter.

20.

"I don't see what good can come of this stupid meeting," Dad grumbled as he drove them over to the church. Pastor Vincent had recommended they meet on neutral turf, and although Dad had reluctantly agreed, Sophie knew he was miffed to be torn from his big screen, brewskies, and football games.

"It might help to get things out in the open," Mom said.

"Who wants things out in the open?" Dad said as he turned into the parking lot. "Back in my day, they used to just sweep this kind of thing under the rug."

"Times have changed, Bud. Besides, our family isn't the only one affected by this."

"You really think this is going to rock the Morrises' boat?" Dad pulled into a spot and turned off the car.

"Probably more than you know." Mom got out of the car.

He grunted. "I doubt that it's even a blip on their radar scale. You ask me, they just want us here for some public humiliation, so they can look down their pious noses at us."

"Dad, I'm really sorry to drag you through this," Sophie said quietly from the backseat.

"It's okay," he said gruffly. "I'm a big guy, I can take it."

As they got out of the car, he put an arm around Sophie's shoulders and gave her a comforting squeeze. "I'm sure it's not easy for you either."

Sophie tried not to look too shocked at this unexpected show of affection. "Let's just get it over with," she told him. "In and out."

He nodded. "Works for me."

"You two coming?"

Sophie's heart was beginning to pound as they entered the building. With each step toward the conference room where they were meeting, it pounded harder. Finally she had to stop in the hallway just to catch her breath.

"Are you okay?" Mom asked.

"I think I'm having a panic attack." Sophie leaned over and clutched her middle. "Or else going into labor."

"Just breathe," Mom said.

"We should go home, Barb." Dad's voice softened. "Why should Sophie be tortured like this?"

Mom didn't respond, and Sophie slowly stood up. "No, it's okay. I'm okay. Let's just do this and get out of here."

But when they were seated across the long table from the Morrises, with Pastor Vincent at the head, Sophie was afraid she was about to lose her lunch. Her head knew that she was done with morning sickness, but her stomach wasn't convinced.

"We all know why we're here today," Pastor Vincent began. "I'd like to start this meeting with a prayer."

Dad grunted ever so slightly, but he at least bowed his head. Sophie was thankful for this moment. Not only for the prayer's sake but also so she could gather her wits. She had barely glanced at Dylan when she came in and had been relieved to see that his head was hanging down. Was it possible that he was ashamed? She hoped so.

Pastor Vincent finished his prayer, then turned to the Morrises. "Let's begin with this side of the table. Jeff, would you like to speak?"

Mr. Morris cleared his throat. "As head of this household, I would like to be the first one to offer my sincere apology." He looked directly at Sophie's dad. "I can't even imagine how your family is suffering thanks to my son's irresponsible behavior, and I am deeply sorry. I hope you can find it in your heart to forgive him—and us—someday."

Dad looked surprised but nodded.

"And Sophie." Mr. Morris looked at her now. "I understand that you had made a purity pledge to God and that you had kept and had intended to keep that pledge. But I also understand that my son pressured you to break this promise . . . and I cannot even tell you how much that shames me. This is not how we raised our son."

"That's right," Mrs. Morris chimed in. "We taught Dylan right from wrong. He grew up in the church. He knows what the Bible says. He had made a purity pledge too. But it's harder for a young man. Girls pursue him relentlessly and—"

"Lynn," her husband interrupted sternly. "Do not defend Dylan."

"That's right," Pastor Vincent said. "Dylan has confessed to his sin. For you to rationalize or excuse his behavior will only set him back."

"But he's a good boy," she protested.

"And Sophie is a good girl," her dad shot back. "She's an honor student. She's the editor of her school paper. She's never given us a moment of grief . . . until *this*."

"That's right," her mom agreed. "She's on the yearbook staff. She was probably going to get lots of academic scholarships for college. She's been a good Christian and gone faithfully to church for years now."

"Even though her parents are *heathens*," Dad said.

"I am not a heathen," Mom retorted.

"I think what we are saying," Pastor Vincent interjected, "is that Sophie is a good girl who had her whole life ahead of her. But she made a mistake. And Dylan is a good guy who also made a mistake. In all fairness, Dylan instigated the mistake."

"And his mistake is what got my daughter pregnant!" Dad slammed his fist on the table. "We can all sit here until the cows come home yapping about forgiveness and goodness, but it ain't gonna change a flipping thing. My daughter will still be pregnant. Her life will still be ruined." He pointed his finger at Dylan. "I hope you know, boy, that it's taking every ounce of my self-control not to leap across this table and throttle you royally. And you just sit there in your preppy little sweater,

232

with your fifty-buck haircut, acting like you're not even here. Like you're making plans about what you're gonna do when you get back to your preppy little school. Maybe you're going to knock up another poor girl."

"Dad!"

He didn't even look at Sophie. "What I want to know, young man, is *what do you have to say for yourself?*" His voice was so loud that Sophie figured everyone in the building could hear him.

Dylan looked up, and Sophie was surprised to see that he didn't look anything like he'd looked last summer. Today he seemed scared and pale and sort of wimpy. "I—I'm sorry."

"That's it?" Dad shook his fist at him. "'I'm sorry'? You think that's going to fix everything? You think that's going to give my daughter her life back? How would you like to be in her shoes, young man? How would you like to walk around with all your friends staring at your big fat pregnant belly?"

"Bud." Mom put her hand on his arm. Not that he was paying any attention. His eyes were still fixed on Dylan, his anger aimed like a shotgun at Dylan's head. Sophie almost felt sorry for him. Almost.

"No, you don't have to worry about that, now do you, boy? The guy gets off easy. Take what you want and then take off on your merry way. You have your fun and leave a big fat mess behind. And you expect the girl to clean up. Well, you may be a Christian, but my moral standard is a heck of a lot higher than yours!" Dad stood, his face red with rage. "Well,

I've had my say now. All I want is to get out of here." He shoved the chair back so hard that it crashed into the wall. Then he turned and stomped out of the room.

"I'm going to go talk to him," Mr. Morris said.

"No!" Mrs. Morris said. "He might kill you."

Sophie's mom actually laughed. "His bark is worse than his bite. Besides, if he was going to kill anyone, it would probably be your son."

Now it was just Pastor Vincent, the moms, Dylan, and Sophie . . . and the room was silent.

"So, Dylan," Pastor Vincent began, "do you have a response to that?"

Dylan looked down at the table.

"Dylan?" his mom persisted.

"I said I'm sorry. I really don't see what more I can do."

"I'll tell you what you can do, son," Sophie's mom said in a firm tone. "You can look my daughter in the eye and say you're sorry. And say it like you mean it, or don't say it at all."

Pastor Vincent nodded. "Good advice."

Sophie watched as Dylan sat there staring at his hands on the table. Part of her wanted to run from the room. But another part of her, a stronger part, just sat there staring at him. Finally he looked up. "I'm sorry, Sophie."

She swallowed hard. "I'm sorry too, Dylan."

His shoulders relaxed ever so slightly. Like he was off the hook.

"I'm sorry I ever met you," she continued. "I'm sorry I fell for your lies. I'm sorry I let you talk me into something that I really didn't want to do. I'm sorry I believed you when you told me I wouldn't get pregnant. I'm sorry I trusted you to have adequate birth control. Mostly I'm sorry that I broke a promise to God."

Mrs. Morris pointed a finger at Sophie. "You make it sound as if you bear no responsibility in all of this. As if Dylan raped you. As if you're the helpless victim."

"Dylan didn't rape me," Sophie told her. "But I did tell him to stop the first time. I told him no, but he didn't listen."

"And the second time?" Mrs. Morris's eyes were like drills.

Sophie sighed, then looked directly at Dylan. "By then I knew I had broken my vow to God. I felt terrible, guilty, disappointed, dirty . . . but then Dylan would come along. He would smile at me. He'd take me in his arms. He'd kiss me and tell me that everything was fine and that he loved me. I'd never felt like that before. And I believed him. I guess I rationalized that since I'd already blown it, since I'd broken my vow to God, I might as well accept Dylan's love. Of course, I was wrong about that too. Dylan never loved me."

Dylan pressed his lips together and looked down at his hands again.

"So what did you expect?" Mrs. Morris asked Sophie. "Did you think if you got pregnant, Dylan would marry you?"

"Mom!" Dylan turned and glared at his mother.

"Some girls are like that," she said coolly.

"My daughter is *not* like that." Mom's voice was controlled but laced with anger. "My daughter is intelligent and motivated and not the kind of girl who would trap any boy into marrying her."

"I concur," Pastor Vincent said. "That was uncalled for, Lynn."

Sophie's mom reached over and took her hand. "If that's all you two have to say, I think Sophie and I will be on our way." She turned and smiled at Pastor Vincent. "Thank you for arranging this meeting."

As they drove home, Sophie's dad seemed in surprisingly good spirits. "You know, Mr. Morris is a stand-up kind of guy. Too bad his son isn't more like him."

"I think Dylan takes after his mom," Mom said a bit harshly.

"Well, Mr. Morris assured me that he will cover all of Sophie's pregnancy expenses, and he even recommended an adoption attorney."

"But Sophie hasn't made that decision yet," Mom protested.

Naturally this resulted in another argument. Dad felt certain the baby would be better off in a "good home with two mature parents," and Mom wasn't sure she wanted to see her grandchild "given away." Thankfully their disagreement wasn't quite as heated as others had been.

Sophie couldn't help but feel slightly proud of her parents as Dad drove home. Sure, they were a little rough around the edges, but they were good people. And they had stood up for her.

21

When school regrouped in January, Sophie went directly to the pregnancy center, where Mrs. Manchester seemed ready for her. "Leah told us your secret, Sophie."

"So I heard."

Mrs. Manchester smiled. "But isn't it better having it out in the open?"

Sophie shrugged. "In some ways. But it's hard being around my friends. The way they look at me and treat me."

"Believe it or not, they'll get used to it. Oh, things will never go back to normal, but before long, they'll have other things to distract them from you."

"So what are my options here?"

"That depends on you, Sophie. What do you want?"

"To hide out until the baby comes."

"That surprises me."

"Huh?"

"You seem like such a strong person. I had thought you might like to continue with your regular classes and activities. You were doing an excellent job on the school paper."

"But I'm not sure that I can . . . I mean, in my condition."

"You're pregnant, Sophie, not terminal."

"I know, but . . . like, Mr. Young—I know he's disappointed in me."

"That's life. Everyone makes mistakes. Sometimes our mistakes make us bigger people."

Sophie patted her belly. "You can say that again."

Mrs. Manchester laughed. "Well, you'll have to decide what's best for you. But I hope you won't just assume it's to hide out, as you say. I'll admit that's best for some girls. But some are strong enough to continue with their lives. Of course, we'll offer you counseling and childbirth classes, and if you're considering keeping your baby, we offer child development classes and child care." She peered at Sophie. "Have you made that decision yet?"

Sophie shook her head. "Not completely. But I think adoption is the best option for me."

"You're the only one who can make that decision."

"So many decisions." Sophie sighed. "Do you think it would be okay if I hung out at the pregnancy center today, just for the day? To see how it feels, you know?"

"That's an excellent idea."

So Sophie was "one of the pregnant girls." At first there was some disbelief that she was actually pregnant. Some had assumed Leah was lying. But Sophie let them know it was the real deal, and she put them at ease using humor. Even Natasha seemed pleased to have Sophie in their group.

Sophie explained the reason behind her overly personal questions last month. "I never even wrote that follow-up article," she confessed. Although a part of her was ready to write it now. She knew just the angle she would take too. A personal experience story—true confessions of a pregnant honor student.

By afternoon, Sophie was bored with the pregnancy center. She wondered if she really belonged there—at least full-time. She decided to go speak to Mr. Young. She knew his planning period was sixth hour, so she waited until then and went and tapped on his office door.

"Hey, Sophie," he said with a smile. "I missed you in class today."

"I was hanging at the pregnancy center."

"That's what Wes said." He waved her to the chair across from his desk. "Sit down."

"Thanks." She sat down and folded her hands in her lap. "I wanted to try it out—the pregnancy center—to see how I fit in."

"How was it?"

"Okay. I mean, the girls are nice. But it was kind of boring too."

He nodded with a knowing smile. "Are you considering returning to your regular classes?"

She nodded. "It'll be embarrassing for a while. But I can probably get used to it."

"Wes told me that you were considering stepping down from your chief editor position and yearbook. Is that true?"

"I figured you'd want me to step down."

"Me?" He looked shocked. "Why?"

"It seems pretty obvious."

"Do you think being pregnant will impair your work?"

"I don't think so."

"And you were pregnant in the fall, right?"

She nodded.

"If anything, I think it made you a better journalist, Sophie. You were able to see more sides of a story."

"Yeah, pregnancy kind of does that to you. I guess it's the humiliation factor."

He smiled. "So, as far as I'm concerned, you're still chief editor. And you're welcome in any of my journalism classes. In fact, I wanted to ask you to be my AA next semester."

"Really?"

"Absolutely."

She sighed. "Thanks. I'd like that."

As it turned out, Mrs. Manchester was right. After a couple of weeks, Sophie was no longer the center of gossip and attention. For the most part, her life seemed to take on a normal pace. Other than her growing midsection, prenatal vitamins, and OB appointments, life seemed fairly smooth. It still bothered her that almost everyone (except Carrie Anne, who still wasn't speaking to her) assumed that Wes was the father, but he told Sophie to just let it go. When he and Sophie ate lunch with Jenny and Hannah—and even Kelsey eventually—they would affectionately tease him, calling him "Sophie's baby's daddy." And he would just laugh and take it in stride.

Sophie continued to spend some time in the pregnancy center for group therapy sessions and personal counseling, and she signed up for Mrs. Vincent's childbirth class. Sometimes she went there just to visit.

"Leah had her baby last night," Natasha told Sophie in late January. "A boy. Seven pounds, six ounces. Healthy."

"She's still planning to keep him?"

Natasha shrugged. "That's what she's been saying."

"Do you think it's because she hopes her boyfriend will come back to her?"

"She still thinks he'll change his mind in time. But I think he's just like the rest of the guys—making his fast break."

Sophie sighed. "Not all guys are like that."

"No." Natasha made a face. "Your Wes is perfect. He wants to marry you and be a daddy to your kid." She lowered her voice. "But then he's not really the daddy. The real daddy bowed out a long time ago."

"Point taken."

"What is it with guys anyway?"

Sophie chuckled. "You mean besides the fact that most teen guys think with a part of their anatomy that's not even connected to their brain?"

Natasha laughed. "Why don't you write an editorial about that?"

"Maybe I will."

"I heard that your school paper is more widely read than ever this year." Natasha grinned. "That's because you write about things related to sex."

"You mean like pregnancy?"

"Yeah, that's related to sex. But you've written about birth control and abortion too. What about adoption? Why haven't you done that yet?"

"As a matter of fact, I'm working on an adoption article right now."

"You can use my story, if you keep it anonymous."

"Thanks."

Sophie knew that Natasha had made her final decision. Going against her mother's wishes, Natasha was working on an open adoption. Not so much so that she could be involved in the child's life, but because her mother wanted to leave that door open. It was a compromise. The baby was due in early March, and after recovering, Natasha would return to her high school to finish out her junior year. She told Sophie that she might even go to the prom if she was asked. Natasha was so pretty, Sophie thought there was a good chance.

There was no chance that Sophie would attend her prom in early May. Despite Wes's invitation, she had decided that being full-term pregnant in a prom dress was just too much for her. There was only so much humiliation a girl could handle.

❄

Sophie hadn't told anyone, including Wes, that it was her birthday. But on February 12, she turned eighteen. Old enough to vote, be in the armed forces, and have a baby. Oh yeah, a girl could have a baby at thirteen too. She knew this for a fact since a thirteen-year-old had just been admitted to the pregnancy center—the youngest girl there.

On her way to the cafeteria, Sophie felt someone tap her on the shoulder. She thought it was Wes, but to her surprise, it was Carrie Anne. "Happy birthday," she said quietly.

"Hey, thanks." Sophie smiled at her.

"How are you doing?"

"Okay."

"Sophie?"

"Yeah?"

"I'm sorry, okay?" Carrie Anne looked like she was close to tears.

"Sorry? For what?"

"For treating you the way I have. For being such a pathetic best friend."

"It's okay." Sophie put her hand on Carrie Anne's arm. "I know it's not easy being friends with a knocked-up girl."

"Well, God really convicted me," Carrie Anne said. "I know I was wrong. But the truth was, it wasn't just you being pregnant."

Sophie nodded. "I kind of ruined your illusions about Dylan, right?"

"Yeah . . . but you're right. They were illusions." She lowered her voice. "And have you heard?"

"What?"

"He got another girl pregnant."

Sophie blinked. "No way!"

Carrie Anne nodded. "I overheard my parents talking about it. I'm not supposed to know. Can you believe it?"

Sophie sighed. "Unfortunately I can."

As the weather got warmer, Sophie got bigger. By late April, it seemed that every part of her body was screaming. Her ankles were swollen, her back hurt, her bladder was always too full, her breasts were bigger than ever, and the skin on her stomach resembled a road map with the new stretch marks that seemed to pop out daily.

"I wish you could just induce me," she told Dr. Phillips.

"Don't worry, Sophie, it shouldn't be long now."

"That depends on how you define long." Sophie struggled to sit up. "Every day feels like it's about seventy-two hours long now. And I haven't slept a night in weeks."

"Some people say that's nature's way of getting a mother ready for nightly feedings."

"Well, that won't be a problem for me," Sophie assured her.

"So you've made up your mind."

Sophie felt the baby kicking and rubbed her belly. "I was pretty sure all along," she admitted. "But it's still hard. Especially as the baby got bigger. Like she has a personality of her own and everything. Sometimes I can imagine being a mom, and I think I'll be a good one—someday."

"I think you will too."

"But I think the kindest thing for the baby is to be in a loving home with two parents. I've been working with a good attorney, and I know the couple getting my baby is as good as it gets."

"And how do you define that?"

"I know, it's tricky," Sophie said. "My parents are really great. They've actually been really great throughout the pregnancy. I mean, we had our moments, but mostly they're cool. But the parents I picked for my baby have been trying to have kids for years. He's a public defender, and she's a freelance editor who works from her home. And they're Christians."

"Sounds like a good choice."

"I think so." Yet Sophie wasn't sure. What if her child grew up and questioned why her mother had given her up? What if the parents weren't all they seemed to be? What if their marriage was in trouble? What if, like some couples, they got pregnant after adopting and Sophie's baby suddenly became like the redheaded stepchild?

Sophie knew she could ask "what ifs" until her brain burst, but it wouldn't change anything. Mostly she could simply trust her instincts on this and pray. She was committed to pray for her daughter for the rest of her life. And if her daughter ever wanted to meet her or needed to know about her biological roots, Sophie was willing to go there.

❋

"Aren't you glad I didn't let you take me to the prom?" Sophie gasped as Wes drove her to the hospital.

"Keep breathing," he told her. "Like your birthing coach told you to do."

"I am breathing, silly. I'm just not having a contraction right now."

"Oh, okay."

"But can you imagine how embarrassing it would've been if we'd been out on the dance floor and my water had broken?"

He laughed. "Yeah, we would've been the hot topic of the evening."

"It was bad enough having to leave the movie theater. I hope they can get that seat clean—" Suddenly her body was gripped by a giant vise that threatened to squeeze the very life out of her, and the next thing she knew, she was screaming.

"Breathe, Sophie, breathe!"

"Hee hee hee hee," she hissed over and over just like Carrie Anne's mom had taught her to do. She felt like her body was being ripped apart, like someone had taken a hot poker and stabbed her in the back with it. How did women survive this?

After what seemed hours but was truly just minutes, Sophie was being wheeled into the labor room. And that's when the real fun began. Everything she'd felt from the beginning only intensified until she really did believe she was going to die.

"Do your breathing," Mrs. Vincent told her. "Stay on top of it, Sophie."

"Keep it up, sweetie," her mom said, "you're doing great."

Mrs. Vincent squeezed her hand. "This contraction is almost over."

On and on it went until *finally* Sophie was ready for an epidural and a little bit of relief. "I can't believe women actually choose to do this on purpose," Sophie said hoarsely. "I swear I'll never have sex again."

"Childbirth," Mrs. Vincent said, "the best form of birth control."

Sophie sighed and closed her eyes.

"That's right, honey," Mom said, "get some rest."

"Because you're going to need it," Mrs. Vincent added.

And she did need it. It took a full hour of back labor and pushing until she was certain her eyeballs were going to pop out before she heard Dr. Phillips say that the head was emerging. By then Sophie was in so much pain that even the sound of the baby's cries went right over her. Apparently that's when she passed out.

When Sophie came to, she had been moved to a regular room, and all was quiet. She reached down to touch her stomach and could tell that the baby was gone. Not that her tummy was gone—it still seemed abnormally big, only now it was floppy too. And she could tell that the living, moving life-form that had been with her for nine months was no longer there. To her surprise, she began to cry.

"These are from Wes," her mom said as she came in with a bouquet of yellow roses. "And Dad sends his love, but you know how he is about hospitals. Are you okay?"

"I—I think I'm okay. But I miss her."

"You miss her?"

"The baby." Sophie clung to her stomach and cried even harder.

Mom looked shocked. "Do you wish you were still pregnant?"

"No, of course not." Sophie firmly shook her head. "It's just weird. I miss her and I feel sad."

"Do you want to see her?"

Originally Sophie had told everyone that she didn't want to see her baby. She had wanted to have her, sign the papers, and just move on. Now she was unsure. "Maybe so . . ."

Her mom nodded. "I think that's wise, sweetie. She's such a cutie pie too. She looks so much like you did."

Within minutes Sophie was holding her very own baby in her arms. The baby was so perfect, so sweet, so complete, that it took Sophie's breath away. She touched a soft cheek, and the baby turned her head and looked into her eyes. Sophie's eyes filled with tears, and it felt as if someone had just slid a dull knife into her heart. "Here, Mom," she said quickly. "Please, just take her."

"But, honey, that wasn't—"

"Just take her. Now."

Her mom took the baby and left the room. Once again Sophie cried. She sobbed so hard that she got the hiccups. Even then she couldn't stop crying. Why was this so painful? Why wasn't she just relieved? After all, it was over now. For months that's all she had wanted—for it to be over. And now that it was over, she was a basket case.

"Here." Mom handed her a glass of water. "Drink this."

Sophie slowly drank as Mom rubbed her shoulders. "You did good in there, honey. Real good. And it's only natural that you should feel sad now. You're only human, sweetie. If you didn't react like this, I'd wonder where your heart was."

"My heart feels like it's in pieces."

"I know, honey."

"She's so pretty, Mom."

"She is. The attorney told me that the adoptive parents were practically delirious with joy." She pointed to the huge bouquet of gorgeous pink tulips. "That's from them."

Sophie looked at the tulips and sighed. "She'll be in good hands, won't she, Mom?"

"You know she will."

"How big was she anyway?"

"She was nine pounds and seven ounces."

"Wow." Sophie shook her head. "No wonder it hurt so much."

After a short nap, the attorney came in with the final paperwork. As she signed her name, she felt that dull knife slicing through her heart again. "I'm not sure which hurt more," she told him as she handed the papers back, "giving birth or giving her away."

"Are you having second thoughts?" He peered down at her with a creased brow. "Because you don't have to do this, Sophie. I'll admit the adoptive parents would be crushed. But it's your choice, you know that."

"I know." She sighed. "And I know it's the right thing to do. I just didn't expect it to hurt this much."

He made a sad smile. "Maybe that's how God felt."

"Huh?"

"You know, when he gave up his Son."

She considered this.

"It's a huge sacrifice, Sophie. Very unselfish too."

She swallowed against the lump in her throat. "But it's because I love her that I can do it . . . even if it does hurt."

"Unfortunately love hurts sometimes."

She nodded. "You got that right."

❀

Sophie knew she wasn't the same person after going through nine months of pregnancy and giving birth. Oh, sure, she could pretend to be the same funny, witty girl as before, but she knew she had changed. And that was okay. Some of the changes had to do with how she looked at life, and even more how she looked at others. She realized this experience had forced her to grow up—as a human and as a Christian.

Although she felt she'd been forced to grow up a little too quickly, facing questions and decisions that most teens would rather postpone, she still knew that her life as a teenager wasn't over—not like she'd believed it had been before. Because now she knew for certain that God really did give fresh starts. He really did allow "do-overs."

So when Sophie recommitted herself to her purity pledge, she did it in private. And when she felt the reassurance that God was restoring her purity—in his own way—she knew she would keep this moment stashed away deep inside of her. No way was she going to make this a big public show. This time it was a vow between her and God—alone. And this time she knew she would keep that vow. With God's help, she would keep it.

For as long as I can remember, I've been stuck in the middle. Like being dealt a loser's hand with no more turns to take, my luck seemed to run out even before I was born. My older sister, Rose, got all the good stuff. Not only did she get the looks in the family, but being an energetic and fairly demanding child, she got the best part of my parents' attention too. I'm pretty sure this is true, because I've seen all the photos of young Rose with my parents—happy snapshots of the three of them laughing and having fun, all taken before I came along.

By the time I was born, only two years later, my mom was already getting a little worn-out by Rose's antics. And I've heard that my dad was severely disappointed that I was not the son he'd been longing for. If I'd been a boy, I would've been named Norman Nelson Flynn, after my dad, but because I was just another girl, my dad left the name-assigning task to my mother, a frustrated botanist who never graduated from college. Naturally, she decided to call me Aster. This is the name of a common and insignificant little flower that's not very pretty—some people even consider it a weed. Of course, my mom swears she loves asters for their simplicity and hardiness, but I'm still not convinced.

When I was about two, the third baby came along, and if it wasn't bad enough that she was another girl (my dad had already purchased an expensive baseball mitt for her), she also suffered from birth defects. Fortunately for this baby, she was quiet and good-natured, and so soft and creamy-white-looking that my mother named her Lily.

My dad hung around for a few more years, but it was easy to see, even for a little kid, that the man was miserable. I remember trying my best to make him happy. And knowing his aversion to his youngest daughter and her special needs, I would try to humor Lily if she ever cried when he was around. I would even try to act like a boy and play ball with Dad in the yard. But, looking back, I can see now that we were steadily losing him. And just before I turned ten, Dad left our house for work one day and never came back. That's when my mom gave me Lily. "You take care of her," she said that summer day. "She likes you."

That was seven years ago, and it seems like I've been taking care of Lily ever since. It's not that I don't love Lily. I do. But sometimes I just get tired, or, like my mom likes to say about herself, "I'm totally burned-out." Of course, I don't say this back to my mom because that would be like throwing fuel onto the fire. Why go there? But sometimes, and more often lately, I think that I deserve to have a life of my own too.